Whisper in the Dark

by

Dianne McCartney

Whisper in the Dark

Cover Art by *Tina Lynn Stout*

The Wild Rose Press, Inc.
PO Box 708
Adams Basin, NY 14410-0708
Visit us at www.thewildrosepress.com

Publishing History
First Edition, 2024
Trade Paperback ISBN 978-1-5092-5355-5
Digital ISBN 978-1-5092-5356-2

Published in the United States of America

No family. Oh, good. When she disappeared, there would be no whining relatives to complain except Hale and he might even be sick of her by then. He hoped not. Snatching her would be more fun if he pined over her absence. Mulling over the memory of their kiss at the event the other night, he felt certainty turn into doubt about Hale getting bored of her. It took a lot of incentive to make a stick in the mud like Hale make such an amorous demonstration in public.

He continued to read, shocked a few minutes later to discover she already resided in Gideon's home. That was a first, a more esteemed position than any woman in his life had held until now. It solidified the plans for his next attempt at overturning the other man's universe. He would snatch her away from him, take her in every way possible to punish both of them. Any potential schemes concerning the babbling idiot sister fled. Pampered little Tess was a mere child compared to this vital, enthralling woman who represented a worthy challenge. Ethan's perverse energy renewed, he closed the paltry file and headed back downstairs to quell his rapacious appetite once again.

Praise

Dianne McCartney is the author of eight other novels published by The Wild Rose Press.

Dedication

To all the agencies that help keep our world safe.

Acknowledgments

Thanks, as always, to my husband, Mitch, daughter, Colleen and son-in-law, John for their continual support.

I'm also grateful to my wonderful editor, Ally Robertson, and the rest of the excellent team at The Wild Rose Press.

Other Wild Rose Press Titles by Dianne McCartney:

Just One Night
The Daughter of Death
The Road to Justice
Fear the Night
Dark Vengeance
Dark Motives
Dark Venom
Breathing Fire

Chapter One

Gideon Hale thought of the many ways a man could die and wondered which had been selected for him. The ropes that bound him cut off all the blood to his aching hands and feet, making circulation a fond memory. For what seemed like the thousandth time, he wondered who had left him here and why.

This moment marked the seemingly endless middle of the third night unless he had slept for longer than he recalled. In the beginning of this nightmare, he hoped this experience might be a ransom situation, easily solved with a chunk of his fortune. He could always make more money, something that came naturally to him. Only hours ago, however, he'd heard one of the random voices in the background mention disposal. He didn't think they were referring to garbage. If they meant to kill him, why the hell had they left him rotting away up here?

His stomach grumbled again, an almost comical sound in the face of his present predicament. An annoying lack of food didn't pose the biggest threat, of course, but a lack of fluids certainly did. Even he knew a human being would die of thirst long before he dies of hunger. He felt so parched that his tongue sometimes stuck to the roof of his mouth. To add insult to injury, the distinct odor of urine tortured his nose. Humiliation taunted him, a ridiculous, wasted emotion given his current depressing circumstances.

His sister, Tess, would be frantic. He had been on his way to a dinner date with her when the kidnappers snatched him. Four masked men, jumping out of a van, like something on those overly dramatic crime shows that peppered every channel. When such a bewildering trauma happened to you, the entertainment aspect became somewhat diluted.

Although Gideon prided himself on an immense amount of common sense, he found himself initially kicking and hollering like a rebellious toddler. An ingrained fight or flight instinct ran deep. They'd covered his head before dragging him from the van, so he didn't have a clue about his location. He realized after many calls for help that the kidnappers hadn't bothered to gag him because no one could hear his shouts. His attempts had only made them laugh and jeer. All his futile efforts to fight left him with skin scraped raw as well as trickles of blood down his wrists and ankles.

When it became clear his efforts were in vain, he tried to claw his way back to that inherent core of common sense which would allow him to focus on his rather limited options. As precious hours ticked by, the ability to focus his rambling thoughts on anything positive slipped away. He should be thankful he updated his will eighteen months ago. Having finally given up on ever finding a woman to be the love of his life, he'd left everything to the only other woman he loved. Tess would inherit enough cash to do anything she wanted and more, although he knew it would be cold comfort. If they weren't so close, he might have suspected she was behind these evil manipulations. He couldn't think of one other person who would have anything to gain from his demise. It troubled him that, a perennial people person, she wasn't good at being alone. She might have to learn.

His careful estate planning and worries about Tess didn't provide much comfort at the moment as he shivered from the cold. On the other hand, maybe the kidnappers would allow him to snooze through his execution. Is it possible to doze off with a gun in your face, he thought with a morbid twist of humor. Losing consciousness would be an unexpected kindness and a lot more than he had any reason to expect. That last morbid thought became a strange prelude to restless sleep.

Unsure of exactly what woke him a short time later, he blinked awake and struggled to check out his barren surroundings. Rough, slatted wood walls surrounded the space and the floor was cold cement. He'd heard rustling in the shadows he knew were rats or mice. He tried not to think about that. At this moment, the inky black shadows showed nothing but a mere glimmer of wavering light from the window. Thinking it must be moonlight, he waited to see if he could hear anything, holding his breath. He could have sworn the silence was too absolute, then called himself a fool and expelled the air which he'd been holding.

He heard another drawn breath.

One that wasn't his own.

A couple of muffled steps he might have imagined brought a human being to his side. He blinked a few times, certain he'd finally succumbed and lost any sense of reality. The tip of a boot brushed against his hip, a gentle nudge. Incredulity had him straining to see, but the shadows before him only seemed to shift. Even turning to face the now-open window still brought only a diluted streak of light gray, as he squinted at the tall, faint form hovering above him. He struggled to speak. "Wh—"

A gloved hand clamped over his gaping mouth, what felt like leather scuffing his desert-dry lips. "Shut up." Although the harsh words were whispered, he registered a woman's voice. *What the hell.* "We are going to get you out of here. It is essential that you keep quiet. Nod if you understand."

He nodded like a bobble doll, the motion making his throbbing head pound harder. Surviving a headache was doable. Surviving this bizarre moment might be another question.

Looming closer, she continued, "We're leaving you tied up, because I know you can't walk. It will be easier to carry you that way." Gideon nodded his understanding, wondering who the "we" included. She couldn't manage hefting him by herself. He weighed a solid one hundred ninety pounds, maybe a little less after starving for three days. "We have to lower you from a window and you're a big man. It will be easier if I knock you out." He shook his head in protest, once, then again for emphasis. Getting knocked out couldn't be good— he'd already lost all semblance of control. The urge to help save himself hadn't yet died.

"Don't worry," she murmured, passing a stroking, gloved hand over his cheek. That single sensation seemed strangely erotic, here in the dark. "There's just one thing I need you to remember," she added. He tried to meet her gaze, but only saw the shadowed outline of her face.

She moved a little closer in response to his effort.

"Tell your sister, 'Even Steven.' " With gentle care, she put a hand against his neck. He felt one small prick on his skin and everything faded to black.

Chapter Two

The dewy smell and chill of early morning registered first. Gideon eased one eye open and then the other, wincing against the glare of harsh sunlight that inundated his sight. Every muscle in his body tortured him with painful spasms. As he huffed in a breath and tried to stretch, he realized his arms and legs were no longer bound. A jolt of adrenaline made him realize that meant he was truly free. He smothered an emasculating sob of relief.

A faint shuffle at his opposite side jarred him and he struggled to focus through bleary eyes. Expecting to see the woman, he blinked a few times in confusion. He peered up as a threatening hulk of a man squatted beside him, his muscles testing the sleeves of his shirt. When their gazes met, he spoke, the tone of his voice as low as a bass drum. "You're safe at home now, hidden in the trees to the rear of your back lawn. In a few minutes, a call will be made to tell your sister where to find you. They'll come to help you. Do you understand?"

"Yes. Thank you." Gideon's voice creaked and broke like an old man's, the few words all he could gasp at the moment.

The giant man pushed shaggy brown hair out of his dark eyes. A scar ran along one side of his chin, giving him a sinister look that belied his actions. "The story that will be released to the public is going to be that the local police received a tip on where to find you. Parker, the head cop, will take care of all that. Ask him whatever you want. The official version is that you were rescued, but the people who grabbed you escaped."

"I don't understand."

"You don't have to," the other man replied. "You just have to go along with our version. If you tell anyone else the truth, you will be endangering the woman who saved you and the rest of our team. Is that what you want?"

A quick memory hit him then, of that calming hand stroking his face. "No. But my sister—"

"You can tell your sister, but no one else. And the rules apply to her, too." He rose to his impressive height, dwarfing Gideon's own six feet by at least three or four inches. "The bastard who did this to you has a lot more to answer for and his arrest has to be perfectly timed. Don't screw it up." With that, he turned and walked away, surprisingly light on his feet, leaving only the rustle of fallen leaves in his wake.

Gideon lay quietly, every one of his muscles weak and throbbing in protest. For the next three or four minutes, he kept wondering if someone would really come out to help him. Despite devastating odds, he was free. He struggled with a clawing sense of disbelief. Pride had long since abandoned him, so he would crawl if necessary. Crawl for as long as it took. As soon as he managed to drag his enervated body onto the open lawn, surely someone would catch sight of him through the back windows.

His trembling arms and legs still were mostly numb, but needle pricks and jabbing pain promised a return to usefulness in the near future or so he hoped. Such discomfort was a small price to pay for his survival. He strained to detect voices, but heard nothing except the birds chirping in the surrounding trees, their cheery song mocking his uselessness. Growing desperate, he summoned the energy to drag himself down the slope to the back door. He could roll, couldn't he? Maybe he could roll. He'd try anything at this point.

Before he got the chance to try, he heard Tess shrieking his name. Her shrill words grew steadily closer along with her running steps thudding on the lawn. He shouted in response or at least tried his best, his final effort coming out as a muffled grunt she had no hope of hearing. She burst onto the scene, whirling into the small circle of trees like a demented fairy, throwing herself down onto his aching body. He bit back the jolt of pain, patting her slender arm with one hand. "I'm okay, sweetie."

She likely couldn't hear him through the chaotic storm of her tears. Gulping, she tried to catch her breath, staring at him through bleary, red-rimmed eyes. He attempted to pull his legs underneath him, but the arm he used to support himself shook, then gave way.

"Steady, sir." A stocky, blond man, probably in his thirties, strode through the trees and put a hand out to stop him.

Gideon grabbed his arm for support instead. "I take it you're one of the good guys." The rasp of his voice made him sound like a stranger.

"Lieutenant Parker, sir."

"Well, Lieutenant, if you can give me a hand up, and a shoulder to lean on, we'll see if I can persuade my legs to work."

"Should I call for medical assistance?"

"Let's get inside first." With the other man's help, he staggered to his feet, trying to ignore the odd, burning feeling and the cursed shakiness in his limbs. Lieutenant Parker pushed one sturdy shoulder under one of Gideon's arms. Tess, who had finally run out of tears, tried in vain to stretch her five-foot-three to reach him on his other side. He put his hand on her shoulder for support instead.

He felt as weak as a newborn colt, but, once he stood, the welcome sight of his home beckoned through the branches. The other two let him set a slow, stumbling pace. As their awkward group shuffled forward, he could spy Henry, who took care of the house, coming to meet them. He approached with his usual brisk pace, coming to a sudden stop in front of him. His face drawn, he said, "You gave us quite a scare, young man." His sixty-year-old face looked more like eighty, clear evidence of the stress he'd suffered. He took Tess's place as support and she led their odd parade into the house. Gideon staggered like a drunk, even when supported, but they made it inside without further incident.

Finding their way to the living room, they managed to help him get safely seated, wisely putting a throw over the leather chair first. Lieutenant Parker hustled Henry away, ignoring the worried look the older man cast. Every bone in Gideon's body ached as he eased back in his favorite recliner. Tess had to push the recliner control for him. He took a first painful sip of water to soothe his dehydrated throat from a bottle she fetched from the kitchen. "Just sip it, so you don't get sick." She offered to call their family doctor, but they agreed to delay his visit for an hour since Gideon appeared to have survived his ordeal intact.

To their dismay, the first thing he insisted on after a drink was taking a shower. He knew they couldn't possibly understand how filthy he felt. When they protested that he was too weak, he insisted they put a chair in the downstairs shower so he could sit. That done, he waved the others out, summoning Henry to assist him in dragging off the soiled clothes. "Burn them," he muttered, turning away from the smelly heap. The other man whisked them away after dangling the shower attachment down so that he could reach it and giving him a bar of soap and shampoo. Not everyone would understand his immediate need to be clean, but he wanted to feel more like himself and this was the easiest way. The warm, rushing water soothed a few of the aches as well. Showering even from a seated position sapped every bit of energy he had left. After Henry helped him slip on pajamas and a thick, soft robe, he helped him back to the library, then disappeared to give them privacy the lieutenant had requested.

It seemed strange being the one bundled into a chair, a blanket over his knees, as if he was an elderly patient rather than a thirty-nine-year-old man. Swearing, he shifted position with a groan. His body aches and exhaustion aside, his mind, now geared up, refused to slow down. He realized as Tess fussed and clucked over him that it gave her something to do that distracted her. The sooner that they got back to something approaching normalcy, the better.

Peering down the rows of beloved books near where they settled, he sighed. Until now, he hadn't realized how much he would miss the old fieldstone fireplace with the painting of their parents hanging over the mantel. "Lieutenant Parker," he began.

The other man closed the door and crossed the room to take a seat opposite him. "I'm sure you have questions. Ask anything you like, but I may not be in a position to answer."

He nodded. "Fair enough." His sister settled into the chair next to him, her legs curled underneath her. "How much can you tell me about this incident? All I know is that I'm supposed to keep the information between the three of us."

"What do you mean, between us?" Tess cut in.

The police officer grimaced. "I apologize for all the rules. I can tell you we're counting on your discretion. That includes both of you, of course."

"You have our word on it. I'm just relieved to be home." He rubbed his face in an effort to clear his mind of all the memories of his ordeal. "I have to at least know who instigated this mess."

Lieutenant Parker settled back in his chair, folding his hands. "I'm not permitted to share that information with you. I can tell you that it is a competitor you have beaten in the business world. He isn't taking it kindly. This is basically a huge over-reaction to what you probably consider daily life in such a competitive arena."

Tess's mouth gaped in surprise. "We know the man who kidnapped him?"

He leaned over to cradle her hand in his own. "That term, a competitor, doesn't narrow it down much, I'm afraid. Real estate investment is a huge, rather cutthroat business. Here in Chicago, the rules change on a daily basis." A terrifying idea about possible ramifications took hold. "How can I protect Tess if I don't know who did this? What are the odds he'll try again?" He recognized the futility of the question too late, but the

11

other man responded at once.

"I understand your concerns, and they're certainly valid, but it's important that you both continue to act normally. Carrying on with your regular day-to-day lives will convince him that he's got away with it. If this man suspects we're onto him…" He shrugged, but Gideon understood his point. "For the foreseeable future, we will have officers posted close by. With your permission, one agency or the other will provide adequate security when you go anywhere."

Gideon started to say he didn't need any such thing and then realized the irony of his response. He could have used some armed men to accompany him a few days ago. "Okay, I understand. Given what just happened, I think it makes sense to go along with your advice for now. I gather, then, that there are multiple agencies involved."

"Yes. That's because of the number of cases involved and the fact that several different states are included as crime scenes." Relief spread across Parker's face. "I appreciate your cooperation. We know who kidnapped you, but we find ourselves in a difficult situation. This man is also suspected in the murders of five women."

Gideon ignored Tess's gasp. "What on earth could my kidnapping have to do with the murder of five women?"

"The suspect is the only connection." The other man met his gaze. "We think it was an impulse to take you, and, frankly, that's a decision that benefitted us. He's getting cocky after avoiding capture for so long. That arrogance is what caused him to finally make a mistake. To be honest with you, it's the break we've been praying for."

He puzzled over the shocking idea of not one murder, but five, his mind sluggish. "I still don't quite understand how you located me. I think I was somewhere in the country. I couldn't hear any street noise, just a few birds and dogs. The kidnappers didn't seem at all worried when I yelled for help."

Parker glanced back and forth between them. "To be brutally honest, you simply benefitted from a rare bit of good luck. We had a tail on our suspect and he met with a man he shouldn't know unless he was planning a crime of some sort. One of the men that man subsequently hired had a drug habit and loose lips. When we arrested him, he gave us all the information we needed to locate you in exchange for a reduced charge and relocation."

Gideon paused for a moment and realized just how fortunate he had been. "And if you grab him now, you won't get the evidence you need on the other crimes? Is that it?"

Parker nodded, looking relieved that he'd worked it out for himself. "This case has been going on for almost five years. For the first time, thanks to his vendetta against you, we are much closer to catching him. It's necessary, however, to proceed with great care."

"I see." He really did understand—years of intense police work, potentially for nothing. Just the cost of the manpower involved in solving such a case was astronomical. "Am I allowed to ask about the identity of the two people who saved me?"

"I'm afraid not." He smiled. "I'm sorry about that. It's perfectly natural that you would want to know, but we have to protect their identities. All I can tell you is they are members of a government agency trained to assist in difficult cases like this." On receiving a nod of understanding from him, Parker continued. "With multiple agencies involved, everyone agreed a small, experienced team could get you out safely with as little fuss as possible."

"How many people were there, Gid? Just two?" Tess asked.

"I only remember two," he replied. "One who spoke to me before we left the house and one after."

"Yes, a two-person team. I've worked with them before on another case. They're two of the few people I would trust to carry out this kind of rescue." Andrew focused his gaze on each of them in turn. "I need to stress how very important it is that you not speak to anyone outside of this room about any details. Not even Henry. A press release will be made about how the local force assisted in your release. Your only response to questions needs to be, 'No comment.' "

"Will you thank them for me? Those two people and everyone else who helped. And tell them if I can assist them in any way, I will."

"Yes, of course." Parker stood, glancing at his watch. "Staying close to home for the next few days until things calm down will help. Television crews are bound to show up when news of your release hits. There are some media representatives in front of the entrance now but, unfortunately, there's bound to be a lot more coming soon."

Glancing out the window, he continued, "Keep your front gates closed at all times. We'll leave an officer posted there for a few days to help you through the worst of it." He pulled a few business cards out of his breast pocket and handed one to each of them. "If you have questions or any problems, this has all my phone numbers on it. Feel free to use them at any time, day or night. I'll come by tomorrow after you've had a chance to rest and we'll fill out a victim's statement."

Tess accompanied him to the front door and returned at once, her face filled with concern. "You need to see the doctor and get some sleep, Gid. You can barely walk."

"I was exhausted until you guys helped me into the house and, now, I can't seem to wind down. It's the adrenaline, I guess. My mind keeps stuttering through the details."

A rap on the door had her standing to answer it. He heard her murmur and Henry's answering words before she closed it again. "The doctor's on his way. You can try to get some sleep after he examines you. I don't want to take a chance on you passing out until you're safely in bed."

"That's a good idea." He knew arguing about it would only upset her, so he didn't bother. She'd been through enough because of him.

Dr. Billings showed up on their doorstep twenty minutes later. The normally quiet man was full of questions about his experience and seemed frustrated at the paltry answers. After Gideon answered what he could, the two of them retired to his bedroom for an examination. Getting there took forever as he toddled along with the doctor's support. He'd never resented the stairs as much as he did today. As expected, after a thorough exam, Dr. Billings only diagnosed dehydration and exhaustion. He kept repeating that it could have been much worse, something of which Gideon was well aware. After confirming exactly what kind of abuse had been meted out, he left instructions to get a lot of rest and drink extra fluids along with a sleep medication in case he needed it. Gideon had no plans to take any unnecessary pills. Medicating himself like that always made him feel fuzzy and vulnerable. That would be especially true now, when his paranoia was at an all-time high. The doctor promised to check in again soon and saw himself out so Gideon could stay upstairs and rest. Sinking onto his bed felt like a gift from the gods. He promised himself that, in the future, he would try to be more grateful for the simple things in life he often took for granted, like a safe place to rest. Moist concrete paled in comparison.

After a few hours' sleep, he woke, feeling a little less shaky. Hobbling carefully down the stairs as he clung to the banister, he settled back in his chair and allowed Tess to pamper him. She answered a quiet knock on the door, retrieved a plate of sandwiches from Henry's unseen hand, and murmured thanks. Crossing the room to place them on the mahogany end table next to him, she said, "You need to eat something substantial. The crackers you had earlier can't have lasted long." She followed her words with a smile, moving her seat farther away to give him room.

He had no appetite, but forced himself to take a small bite anyway. The bread tasted like sawdust in his dry mouth. It was as if saliva had abandoned him for good. He had to be patient. Getting fully re-hydrated would take a few days. Despite his nap, his overall sense of weakness disturbed him. Even lifting the sandwich took effort. His hand trembled. "One of my saviors was a woman," he said, between small, halfhearted bites. Swallowing even that small amount took more effort than it should. He felt the food scrape its way down.

Tess's eyebrows shot up. "A woman?"

"Yes."

"One man and one woman?"

He nodded.

"Did they both carry you?"

Gideon considered her question for a moment, remembering, with a jolt of shame, his aching fear before their arrival, then the subsequent, irrational terror of being left behind. He had never considered himself a pumped-up Alpha male, but his futile efforts to save himself stung. "I think she knocked me out. I felt a sting on my neck and, after that, I don't remember anything until I woke up under the trees."

"What do you mean she knocked you out?" Tess asked, her tone unusually shrill. Her body twitched with excess energy.

He considered the awkward logistics of their escape. "She told me they had no choice, because I couldn't walk or climb down from the second-floor window. And they were right about that. I couldn't even feel my legs." He tried to smile and reassure her. "Every part of me either went numb or was too painful. I felt utterly useless. It wasn't my finest moment."

"Gid," Tess whispered, tears swimming into her eyes. "You can't blame yourself. It wasn't your fault."

He laughed, the noise that came out sounding rusty, as if he hadn't spoken in years. It hurt his throat. "Don't cry now, goofball. The difficult part is over. The entire experience just seemed so surreal." Clearing his throat, he added, "The man was waiting when I came to. He told me help would come after he made a call, then he left." Delayed memory came back, including the soothing hand of the mystery woman and her final words. "She talked to me and touched my face." Suddenly, the distorted pictures in his head cleared. Her exact words flooded back. "Tess, for heaven's sake. That's what I meant to tell you earlier."

"What?"

"The woman's last words to me before she knocked me out were really strange."

"What do you mean by 'strange'?"

Gideon rubbed his head as if to retrieve the memory, but he knew he recalled this part correctly. "The last words she said to me were, 'Tell your sister, Even Steven.'" He could hardly ignore his sister's stunned face. "Does that means something personal to you? Even Steven?"

Tess shook her head, eyes wide, then immediately nodded in contradiction. She perched on the edge of her chair, crouching forward. "I was going to say no, but... well, this is weird. Do you remember me telling you about my college roommate?"

He remembered some half-hearted mention of her. In those days, he had been working eighty hours a week, trying to make a name for himself in the challenging world of real estate. The Chicago business climate stayed competitive, then and now. His parents had still been alive and had kept a closer eye on Tess since he couldn't. A dim recollection surfaced. "You mean the girl who ran away or whatever?"

"She disappeared. Remember? I cried for weeks. She was my best friend and she vanished without a word." Tess sat forward, vibrating with energy. "It seems crazy it could be her, but it's the only way those words make any sense. What exactly did she say?"

He searched his memory for the details of that confusing moment in the darkness. The unforgettable experience came back to him, that odd sense of connection in a simple touch. Mentioning it would be both embarrassing and impossible to explain, so he moved on. "That's really all she told me. She said, 'One more thing. Tell your sister, 'Even Steven.' "

She gasped, nodding her head like a puppet. "It has to be her. No one else would know about that episode. I can't believe it."

"What does it mean? Besides the obvious, I mean. What does it mean to you?"

Tess spoke in a rush, excitement hurrying her words into a babble. "The second day we were roommates, she had these two horrible, slimy guys back her into a corner on her way to class. I saw what happened from farther down the hall and rushed to help her. I hit one of them with that big heavy purse I used to carry, then she kicked the other one in the ankle." She paused to take a breath. "That surprised them so much, it bought us enough time to get away. Ganging together like that made us more than roommates. It made us fast friends. She said one day she would pay me back and we'd be 'Even Steven.' " Her eyes shone with recollection. "She called me Mighty Midget for days after that."

"I don't know, Tess." Thinking about such a strange connection made his head ache and he strained to focus. "It's a bit of a stretch, isn't it? I mean, you haven't seen or heard from this woman in years. Suddenly she pops up out of nowhere to save me?"

"What did she look like?"

He cast back to that fleeting moment, trying to remember any details he could. "In the dark, all I could make out was the outline of her face. She seemed tall, but I was lying down, so I suppose I could be wrong about that."

"She spoke to you, though, right? What did her voice sound like?"

"Low. Kind of husky." He didn't say sexy, but he remembered thinking it.

Tess giggled. "She used to say men raved that her voice was sexy, but other girls said she sounded like a man." Smiling, she leaned over to hug him. "I don't understand how, but I feel certain it's her. That's beyond anything I could have imagined. I wonder where she's been all this time."

"What was her name?"

"Brooklin Mackenzie. But everyone calls her Brook."

Chapter Three

Brook peeled off her battered leather jacket and wandered over to the kitchen sink. By some miracle, there were no dirty dishes waiting. The black greasepaint camouflaging her pale skin would have to be scrubbed off with a scoop of the face cream she kept on the nearby countertop.

It would have been fitting and just that she accompanied Gideon Hale back to Tess's care, but it would have been too risky considering the circumstances. She sighed, turning on the tap. When the water became warm, she added cream and scrubbed her cheeks. Half of the facecloths in her house had become stained with this stuff before she learned to use paper towels and the kitchen sink. Right about the time her skin started to turn from black to irritated red, a brisk knock sounded from the front door. She called out, "Neil?"

"You were expecting the tooth fairy?" Neil's dry response sounded through the door.

Turning off the taps and drying her face, she opened up, gesturing for him to come inside. "That was fast. What—did you just kick him out the car door and keep driving?"

"Yeah. I wanted to stay for a champagne brunch, but you know how it is. I wasn't dressed for company." He snorted a laugh. "Nah, I dropped him on the back lawn under a tree, just like we talked about. Waited by the rear fence line long enough to see the sister race in the right direction." He lumbered in, all six-feet-four of him, and dropped with a thump into the nearest armchair. "Jeez, Brook, I'm gettin' old. Lugging that guy around shouldn't have been so much work. He's big, but he's not a heavyweight like me."

She patted his arm as she walked past him to switch on the coffeemaker. "That's true, but he's not exactly a shrimp, either. If he's doesn't weigh two hundred, he's close."

He grunted, the male sound of it making her smile. "Back in the day, I could lift two of him without a drop of sweat."

"And walk uphill both ways," she teased. The aroma of their brew grew stronger, filtering through the apartment.

He changed his yawn into a scowl. "Watch it, shrimp."

Brook smiled. At five-feet-ten, she could hardly be called a shrimp, but compared to Neil, maybe. She reached up to grab two pottery mugs out of the half-empty cupboard. "You can crash here if you want."

"I was going to work out this morning. Just waitin' to get my second burst of energy." He yawned again and she knew without a doubt that he wouldn't make it to the gym.

She crossed to the sleek coffeemaker she'd treated herself to, then walked over to hand him a newly-filled mug. "You can do a real workout tomorrow. You already did your heavy lifting for the day."

"I like the way you think. Sounds like a plan, I guess." He took a slurp of his coffee and slouched down in the chair, tipping his head back to the headrest and closing his eyes. By the time she fetched his cinnamon roll for him, he'd almost fallen asleep. Setting it down beside his coffee on the side table, she grabbed the fluffy throw off the couch and covered him up, tucking the edges under his muscled arms. Pushing the control for the recliner tilted him farther back. "Thanks, Mom," he mumbled.

She kissed him on the forehead as he drifted off. *Who needs a blood brother when they have a friend like Neil around?* Adrenaline draining, she found her way to her untidy double bed, shoving aside the rumpled covers to climb underneath them. Sleep should have been easy for her, too, but it didn't work out that way. She kept imagining the scene at the Hale house. *Could Tess sleep, or would the anxiety from the last few days keep her on alert? Would Gideon keep his mouth shut?* Instinct told her he would. He couldn't have become so successful in the business world if he didn't practice discretion. More immediate needs overcame her curiosity. Sleep stole over her as she lay listening to Neil's reassuring snores from the other room.

Later, after she rose and ate lunch, he finally woke up long enough to drive safely home. They would return to their jobs tomorrow, so she spent the rest of the day working out and doing long neglected household chores. A domestic person she would never be, she admitted with a sigh, after washing the fourth load of piled up laundry. Her apartment was Spartan and, lately, she'd been thinking rather soulless as well. She'd never owned a real home. She'd lived in plenty of houses, of course, but no one would ever mistake them for the kind of home you see in Christmas commercials. She hadn't suffered, at least from a material standpoint, so that was something she would always appreciate.

When her parents were killed in a car accident, her two-year-old toddler self was sent to live in her uncle's mansion. He did his duty, which she heard him announce daily to whoever was in earshot, but a small herd of governesses and nannies raised her. When they bragged about her intelligence, he would agree heartily that she must be smart, as if he had anything to do with it. At the age of eighteen with excellent grades, university beckoned and she never looked back. She'd earned a full ride scholarship, enough to get out from under her uncle's thumb.

No, the only real family she had ever claimed besides Neil was five-foot-three Tess Hale, the sweetest person Brook had ever met. She'd made a lovely balance with her own practical, somewhat cynical self. Freshman year in college marked the first time she was really happy, hanging out with bubbly, ever-optimistic Tess. Matched in a university office, a true case of opposites attract developed into a subsequent friendship. It was still the closest friendship of her life besides Neil. Walking away from her without a word constituted the hardest decision Brook ever made.

However, when the united intelligence agencies first approached her about this new unit, the possibilities intrigued her. A unit that specialized in serial murderers was a rare thing back in those days, especially one made up from members of multiple agencies. Not to mention one that welcomed female agents. Her superiors wanted her in on the ground floor, both for her advanced computer skills and the fact that she spoke five languages fluently. Until then, the fact that government groups like the CIA and the FBI often recruited right out of college had escaped her notice. The specific job they offered provided a sure way to make a difference in the world and, in some ways, gave her a different sort of family, like Neil. An orphan, too, he'd had a much harder life than hers, but their shared experience of being orphans gave them a common bond. The powers-that-be had insisted on one thing. Cutting all ties before she joined the team was essential to their security.

She had always kept watch over Tess and her very successful brother from afar. When this kidnapping took place, she had been the one to steamroll the rescue attempt. They were lucky, so lucky, that Andrew Parker, an ex-Seal team leader whom she'd worked with before, now worked in the local police department. They'd found a workable solution together and ironed out the details while the men in charge wasted precious time second-guessing themselves. In the end, they just rubber-stamped the rescue and left the details up to the three of them which had worked out well.

She wondered whether Neil would come over later and hang out with her as he often did. As unimpressive as her digs were, his were worse, basically one large, stark room. It stayed clean enough, because he never did anything but sleep and watch television there. The meals he ate were almost always takeout. He squirreled away his money like he didn't know if he could pay for his last meal, but she recognized it as an orphan's habit. In the foster system, you might get shifted to a new home any day, so hoarding what you had provided a necessary, reassuring safety net. That last consideration percolated in her dreams throughout the night.

The next morning, every local news service headline screamed of Gideon Hale's salvation. Stories saturated each broadcast. The snatch and recovery of a local man, successful and well-liked, made great copy for drama seekers. It didn't hurt that he was a very handsome man which surely made his tale popular with female readers. Pitch black hair and brilliant blue eyes could have put him on a fashion magazine. Add on an attractive, fit body and game over. Brief on-camera appearances showed him looking more rested, repeating, "No comment," over and over, obviously trying to be both patient and polite. All the ruckus couldn't have been much fun, but better that than dead.

Attractive looks ran in the family, she mused, because the camera had always loved Tess. She switched off the television. *Time to head to the office.* Sliding her gun into the holster under her arm, she grabbed her keys and a small purse before heading out the door.

****

Henry escorted Dr. Billings in to check up on his patient once again. They went upstairs for privacy. As expected, the physician announced that Gideon was still overtired and a little dehydrated, but, other than that, appeared to be making progress. Gideon couldn't help thinking that progress wasn't fast enough for his comfort. And if they could have found a cure for his leftover nerves, he would appreciate it. After the doctor left, he enjoyed a long, hot shower. It amazed him how grateful he felt for the basics of life, like hot water and soap. The state he'd come home in still taunted him. After he'd toweled off, he dressed and went downstairs. After another small bite to eat and drink, he returned to his room and, once again, fell into an exhausted sleep. It seemed to be all he did these days.

The next day, Gideon sighed as he stared out the

front bay window, watching the throngs of strangers crowded by his front gate. Impossible to tell if they were all newspeople or some were just gawkers. He'd hoped they would have given up by now. The reporters should have moved onto other stories. A stalwart policeman outside of the wrought iron barrier clearly tried to encourage the interlopers to leave, gesturing them to move back to no avail. "Let's make sure to send that poor officer some lunch, Tess. He's more than earning his keep, that's for sure."

"Henry's been bringing him food quite frequently. He feels sorry for him. So do I." She moved to his side and looked for herself. "I guess Lieutenant Parker hoped that if the reporters saw you in person, they might give up and go away."

He grimaced. "No such luck. You'd think they'd have better things to do with their time. A lot of good causes could certainly use that kind of enthusiastic coverage."

"Did Enid cancel your meetings for this week?" She patted the head of their Labrador retriever, Abe, who had finally stopped barking at the intruders. Still upset, he let out a little growl, deep in his throat.

"It's okay, Abe. I know exactly how you feel. And yes, she cancelled my meetings for today and tomorrow. Hopefully, that will be long enough for everything to calm down." He glanced over at Tess, who now sat with her legs curled under her, looking pensive. "What's wrong?"

"What if they come back? What could we possibly do to stop them? One policeman can't keep them out."

It took him a minute to work out that she was talking about his attackers, not the news people. "The

27

kidnappers? Oh, Tess, don't worry. Parker and the other policemen seem to have everything, including our safety, well in hand."

"You say not to worry, but we don't even know what the kidnappers look like. They could look like anyone." She brushed away an escaping tear. "I couldn't bear it if anything else happened to you."

"Nothing else is going to happen to me." Now wasn't the time to tell her he had the same worries about her.

"You don't know that." She stayed silent for a moment, then peered up. "What did you think about?"

"When?"

She glared at him the way only an annoyed woman can manage. "When you were lying there, tied up and hungry."

"More thirsty than hungry, actually. There's nothing like being kidnapped to ruin your appetite." He didn't want to dwell on his time in captivity. It made him feel weak and powerless, which, in turn, embarrassed him. Why did men always think they were safe in public? He was fit and he hadn't had a prayer defending himself against four determined men.

She cursed at his joke, her white-washed version of a worse word, and the rarity of that made him smile. "Actually, I remember being glad that I updated my will." As soon as he uttered that bald response, he regretted it, because, now, there were a lot more tears trickling down her face. "Oh, Tess, seriously, please don't cry. I just made a bad joke. Your tears are more than I can handle after this nightmare."

She sniffled, dabbing away the random drops with a hankie. "My imagination gets away from me, sometimes. I always wonder what was worse—my bad dreams or your reality."

Time to distract her. Dwelling on it won't help either of us. "Honestly, you would have laughed at me. I kicked and swore as loud as I could, like a little kid having a tantrum. What a horrendous waste of energy." He chuckled, although it had hardly seemed comical at the time. "Even when it didn't work, I kept kicking, swearing and tearing my wrists to pieces. Even when I could feel blood running down my fingers." He shook his head, sighing. "So stupid. I totally lost control of my emotions."

"You had to try. I would have done the same thing." Her voice quivered with the admission.

"I realized after the fact that the kidnappers knew no one could hear me. That's the reason nobody gagged me. It took me a while to figure that out." He rubbed his face with both hands, wishing away the annoying, persistent fatigue. "They kept me somewhere pretty private, I guess. In the country, maybe, although Parker never confirmed the location."

"I kept dreaming of all the dreadful things they might do to you. The police said someone would call at some point with a ransom demand, but they never did. That made it so much worse." She cleared her throat and hugged herself, one arm wrapped around the other. "I would have given them every single penny I had, but they never gave me the chance. That made it so much worse. I couldn't stop crying—I'm such a baby."

"No, you're not, but you'll always be my baby sister." He leaned over to brush her bangs out of her face. "I wasn't any big tough guy, believe me. Everything happened in such a surreal way. With the sluggish way I reacted, I should have signed up for a remedial self-defense class." Getting some skills in that area might not be a bad idea. Maybe then, he would have had a chance of protecting himself.

"You never really told me the details. The witnesses only said men dressed in black with guns which was no help at all. None of the people nearby could even agree on how many assailants there were." She shrugged. "The police said that's not uncommon, but it wasn't much comfort."

He took a seat opposite her. "A white paneled van roared up the street, then jerked to a halt a dozen feet in front of me. Suddenly, the door flew open and four of them leapt out. I stood there, motionless, probably with my mouth hanging open like an idiot." He sighed at the thought of his delayed response. "I only had time to think about calling nine-one-one before one guy charged me and threw a massive punch, right to the jaw. I don't think I even raised my hands to try and defend myself."

"Give yourself a break. You were in shock. Anybody would have been slow to react."

He nodded. She had a point. "I guess I should be glad they didn't use their guns. They looked like bank robbers or something. I never dreamt they were coming for me."

"Why would you? There was no reason to worry until he hit you."

"When someone rushes up to you, dressed like that, it's never going to be a good thing." He shrugged. "Anyway, after they threw me inside the van, they sped down the street like a shot. I could hear car horns blaring. Two of the men bound my wrists behind me with some kind of plastic strap, like a zip tie. It cut into my skin."

When nerves started traveling up his back, he took a breath to try and relax. "I remember rolling around a bit, then they pinned me down and tied my legs, too, so I'd stop trying to kick them." He chuckled. "I remember being pleased with myself because I kicked one of them in the privates. Believe me, that pleasure didn't last long." He didn't confess to her that his target had paid him back with a punch that had him curling on the floor in pain. Worrying for hours about them rupturing his spleen had been more than adequate payback.

Tess wrapped her arms around one of the plush pillows from the couch, hugging it, a comforting gesture from childhood. "I tried to call you when you didn't show up at Salvatore's."

"I remember hearing the cellphone ringing and knowing it was you. They threw the damn thing out the window after that. Probably worried about the police tracking it." It had been awful to think about how frightened she would be and how alone in the world if they'd killed him. It made food for thought. Tess had never been happy on her own. Unlike him, she always enjoyed having people around her.

"You've never been late to meet me." She bit the edge of her lip. "I panicked a bit, I guess. I kept envisioning a car accident, crumpled fenders, crumpled brother, you know. Never that you were kidnapped. Something like that never even crossed my mind."

"Of course not. Kidnapping is something you see on the news. It's not the kind of thing that happens to regular people like us. At least, I didn't think it did." He tried to imagine how he'd feel if the situation was reversed. "How did you find out what happened?"

"Henry called and lied by saying you'd been

detained, that I should sit tight. I ordered a drink and played on my phone. Half an hour later he showed up. He and the head waiter hustled me into a back room so the other diners wouldn't see me have a breakdown." She sighed. "Turns out, the other diners missed quite a show. I pretty much lost my mind."

"Oh, Tess, I'm so sorry."

She made a sound that morphed into a chuckle. "Yes, because this is all your fault, right?"

He grinned. "That's better. I'm happier when you're mouthy and sarcastic."

"I was mad at him for lying to me. Isn't that insane? I felt so bad about it later, I just kept apologizing, over and over again." She met his gaze. "We were so lucky," she whispered, her smile cracking along with her voice.

Guilt plagued him about the way she had suffered because of him. He stood and leaned down to hug her, relishing the familiar, comforting scent of her cologne. "You bet we are. Lucky because you've got friends in unexpected places." He walked over to close the drapes against the intruders by the gates.

Chapter Four

Neil and Brook sat slumped in front of the television at her apartment, munching potato chips as he surfed from channel to channel. "Did you hear the boss bragging about how Gideon should thank him in cold, hard cash? Said he could use a new sports car."

Brook nodded. "What a jerk. But that's pretty typical of what we expect from him, isn't it." Their new boss had proven to be a disappointment. He had very few interpersonal skills. They had been spoiled by the many obvious talents of their previous boss who had recently retired. Hopes of getting an equally qualified superior had been instantly dashed the moment the new guy opened his mouth. He had virtually no field experience and it showed.

"Maybe he won't last in a supervisory position much longer."

Talk about optimistic. "Your mouth to God's ear, as they say. We can always hope, but we all know how internal politics work."

Giving up on the depressing subject, they settled on a mystery movie, not surprisingly their favorite genre. "You never told me how pretty your friend is," Neil muttered after a few minutes, staring at the screen.

His use of the word friend threw her for a second. She looked at him in surprise. "You mean Tess?"

"Not like you got a lot of girlfriends to choose

from."

She hid a smile. "Maybe I've got pals from sewing circles you don't know about."

He smirked. "Yeah, because you're so domestic and all," he said in a teasing falsetto.

A laugh bubbled out of her and she threw a pillow at him. "You saw her on the news?"

"Yeah. She looked like a tiny doll next to her brother."

"Tess is girl-next-door beautiful. She's the innocent kind with curly hair and big blue eyes all the guys want to bring home to momma. If I were a betting woman, I'd bet she's busy re-decorating her house and baking cookies." She struck a pose. "Just like me."

He shook his head. "Not so much. You're the kind of girl who makes most mommas quake in their over-protective boots."

"Oh, thanks. Actually, I pretty much feel like a man next to Tess. She's so feminine."

"Don't be an idiot. You'd have to chop off a lot of your lady parts to ever look like a man."

Brook laughed. "Thanks…I think." A statement like that was about as close as Neil ever came to flattery, so she'd take what she could get. Settling back, she added, "I mean she's little and sweet. It's impossible for me to be either."

"True. People like us don't have much experience with sweetness and we weren't little, even at birth." He shifted in his seat to put his feet on the scarred oak coffee table. "According to my sources, she and her brother are supposed to attend some big charity shindig this weekend. First time they've been out of the house."

"How the hell did you find out about those plans?"

Everyone told Neil gossip because they knew he could keep his mouth shut.

He shrugged. "I keep my ear to the ground. One of the guys on their security detail mentioned it."

"I bet they won't attend. Parker told them to lay low for a while."

"I guess a few days is long enough. Gideon confirmed for both of them today. Apparently, it's for one of his favorite charities." Neil studied his fingernails, a telling pose. It was what he always did while he made plans to do something unexpected.

"What's rattling around in that rebellious brain of yours?"

He turned to meet her gaze, lifting one eyebrow. "I guess this shindig attracts a lot of big names. I'm sure that event will need some extra security, don't you?"

She caught his drift, well-used to how his mind worked. "Do you have a tuxedo in your closet, Neil?"

"I can probably rustle one up."

****

Diamonds were the theme for this charity dinner and dance for a well-known, local literacy foundation. Whatever team of volunteers had decorated the room had done a credible job, although everything shone a bit too much for both Gideon's taste and his tired eyes. The white tablecloths and towering crystal centerpieces reminded him of chunks of ice with about as much warmth. He had, of course, complimented the ladies in charge on the décor, as was expected. They twittered and flirted in response. He felt guilty that it all just made him feel like he should have stayed home in front of the fire. But, tonight, he had a particular goal in mind.

The packed room hemmed them in on every side, as

did the hordes of cheek-kissing guests. Noise from all the conversation and the band's background music made his head ache. He noticed Tess, standing at his side, seemed a little tense. "Are you feeling okay? You seem ill at ease."

She scanned the crowd, standing on her tiptoes to peer in all directions. "I'm searching for anyone who looks like a bad guy," she whispered, leaning close to be heard. "But these days, everyone looks suspicious to me, especially if I didn't like them in the first place. Then I wonder if it could actually be someone we like and, somehow, that's worse."

"One way or the other, they're going to get caught." Continuing their casual lives would be difficult if they didn't. He squeezed her hand. "We won't stay very late. I just wanted to make an appearance." A little white lie, he thought, with a twinge of guilt. "And, don't worry. Parker said extra security would be here tonight and we should just enjoy ourselves."

"Oh, great," she answered. "Now, I'll be trying to figure out who the undercover officers are, too. Why is it I feel like I should have taken martial arts classes? If those men tried to take you again, right now, I couldn't do anything to help you."

The idea of his tiny sister using karate on a much larger, muscled creep dredged up a smile. "You didn't even bring a heavy purse you could use as a weapon," he joked, trying to allay her fears.

She glared at him and straightened the strap on her stunning red, floor-length gown. "Don't look now, but here comes a familiar bimbo with your name tattooed on her head. You're the one who might need to borrow a big purse to fight her off."

Turning to see who was approaching, he braced himself for the onslaught of Candee van Burell, who was indeed a bimbo, a rich one, the pampered only child of the most influential banker in town. Dressed in sparkling silver head-to-toe, her plunging neckline showed every asset available for purchase. Salon blonde hair lay lacquered in place. Her over-scaled diamond earrings probably caused the coquettish tilt of her head.

"Darling, we were so worried you wouldn't survive your ordeal." She clung so hard to his arm that he winced from the scrape of impossible talons she called fingernails. "You must tell me all about it. They only reported some boring drivel that gave nothing away in the newspaper." Giving an exaggerated pout, she waited for his response, batting her eyelashes like butterfly wings.

Gideon had learned years ago how to distract Candee and her ilk. He scanned her asset-baring dress. "You look lovely tonight. Doesn't she, Tess?"

Tess offered all the platitudes, making a clownish face when Candee looked away, barely acknowledging her. He smothered a chuckle. "Who are you here with? I haven't seen your father around tonight."

"Daddy's in Europe, silly. I'm here with Ethan."

"Did I hear my name?" Ethan Ames came to stand beside her, his dark brown, silver-threaded hair and blue eyes a model-like complement to her fair complexion.

Gideon had never taken a liking to Ethan, who conveyed arrogance, a sense of entitlement and not much else. Society insisted on manners, however. He nodded a greeting. "Ethan, I believe you've met my sister, Tess?"

****

Neil and Brook observed from across the crowded

ballroom, speculating about how much cash was represented by the attendees. Neil's rogue figure looked unexpectedly dashing in a classic black tuxedo, Brook realized, before turning her attention back to the group containing her friend. She purposely didn't focus on Ethan, afraid her revulsion might show in her face.

"I don't like the look of that," Neil murmured, tipping his head toward the group.

Brook tried to ignore the recurring itch caused by her blonde wig and recalled his earlier remark describing Tess as being pretty. She took Neil's arm, steering him to another corner. "Don't worry. He won't try anything here."

"You hope. He's a brazen son of a bitch."

She shook her head and then pushed the irritating prop glasses farther up her nose. "I know, but he'll need some time to regroup and locate some better thugs." The two of them disappeared back into the crowd. Constantly changing position kept the attention off them.

They spent the next few hours sliding away from Gideon and Tess, but always keeping them in view. The invitations they'd brought, finagled from an acquaintance, showed bogus names, as always. This time they had played with the names Ginger Rogers and Fred Astaire as a joke. They didn't dance together, though. That might strain their cover, considering Neil's notorious two left feet.

She kept her eyes focused on Gideon and Tess, waiting for Neil to use the facilities. When the crowd moved again, she lost sight of them and finally saw Tess, standing much too close to Ethan. She focused on them, ready to intervene if necessary. When someone tapped her on one arm, she assumed it was Neil. "I almost lost them for a second," she said and turned to look right into the dark eyes of Gideon Hale.

"Excuse me. Have we met?"

Her mind scrambled for something to say as her gaze took in the delicious closeup of Tess's brother dressed in a designer tuxedo, his intent gaze focused on her. She raised the pitch of her voice, adding a flirtatious air. "Oh, I'm sure I'd remember that. I'm Ginny Rogers."

He inclined his head, his expression unreadable. "Gideon Hale."

Neil emerged from the crowd and inched in between them. "Sorry I kept you waiting."

She read the expression on Gideon's face and knew he had recognized Neil. There was a tense three-second beat, then he smiled. He reached out his hand. "I'm in your debt," he said as Neil shook his hand. Offering a slight bow in her direction, he backed away, crossing the room to return to Tess's side.

"We're losing our touch," Neil whispered.

"I read somewhere that he has a genius level IQ. That means he's smarter than most of the people we deal with. Don't worry. He won't say anything." They continued to watch the interaction between their nemesis, Ethan, and the other people at the soiree. Many people seemed charmed by the man's looks and his polished manners, but body language spoke volumes. She could tell Gideon and his sister weren't impressed; they slipped away from him as soon as an opportunity presented itself. The two of them didn't know what that monster was capable of, but their instincts were dead to rights. They took great pains to stay on the opposite side of the room. Both brother and sister left shortly after dinner, accompanied by the agreed upon security team.

Staying in the background, she and Neil watched as the duo made their way safely into their limousine. As soon as it pulled into traffic, they breathed a sigh of relief.

"Let's get out of here," Brook said. "These damned high heels are killing me." Thirty minutes later, they ended up landing back at Brook's place just before midnight, their tired, throbbing feet propped up side-by-side on the coffee table. She wiggled her toes, grateful to be out of those torture devices she hoped to never wear again. "Why do you think Gideon insisted on going to that gala tonight? It's not as if he enjoyed it. He didn't dance at all and barely touched his dinner."

"I think he's trying to figure out who his kidnapper is."

She nodded, sighing. "That's what I thought, too. The last thing we need is having some well-meaning amateur detective underfoot."

"You can't really blame him. He's worried about his sister's safety more than his own. I'd do the same thing in his position, wouldn't you?"

"I guess that's true." She stretched the kinks out of her calves. "I don't think Ames is going to give up, do you?"

"I doubt it. Despite Gideon's rescue, he feels untouchable now. That's what happens when you get away with taking peoples' lives. We're going to have to come up with a plan to prove him wrong."

"Do you really think he'll go after Hale again with all of the extra security around?"

"I hope not, but I'm afraid he might see it as a challenge. And we can't take a chance on Tess being victim number six." She rubbed her face and, glancing at her watch, drank the rest of her beer. "Bunking in the guest room?"

"Yeah, if that's okay."

"Any time." Standing up, she leaned down to kiss his cheek. "See you in the morning."

****

Early the next day, the four chastised kidnappers stood with their heads bowed, listening as Ethan ranted and raved. He knew they were smart enough to realize their punishment wouldn't end anytime soon, and would end, if they were lucky, with only threats. Staying silent, they watched him as he paced back and forth. He relished the fear in their eyes and wished he'd thought to put a plastic tarp down for them to stand on, so they'd think about the possibility of blood splatter. "I had to listen to everyone fawn over that bastard last night. It was sheer torture and so unnecessary. Four of you losers guarding one of him and he strolls out of there like he needs some fresh air. Morons! Cretins!"

The boldest of them protested. "He didn't walk out of there. He couldn't have. We had him trussed up so tight he couldn't budge."

He stopped pacing to glare at the man who would dare interrupt him. "You say he couldn't budge? So, what, a guardian angel appeared out of thin air and scooped him up? Or, did he sprout wings?"

This time, no one spoke. They probably realized anything they said would only engage his temper even more. He jerked one hand through his hair, planting himself in front of his sickening band of screw-ups. "If any of this fiasco comes back on me, you're dead men. Do we understand each other? You're as dead as Hale will be when I'm done." They all nodded, then hastily escaped when he pointed at the door. Even the sound of their dirty boots scraping on the floor annoyed him.

Ethan stopped to stare out the window, seeing nothing but a reel of frustrating images that taunted his imagination. All he could focus on was that uppity prick Hale trying to grab every decent property in sight, stealing business away that rightfully belonged to him. He should have been rotting in a grave out back by now with the others. If it hadn't been for the huge police presence after his kidnapping, he would be. Ethan couldn't take a chance of either he or his men getting caught with a corpse. If the plan had been carried out as it should have been, then, maybe by this time, he might have had Gideon's sister on her back for added measure. His latest potential prize—the irritatingly adorable Tess Hale. *Wouldn't that have been tasty?* Now everything was ruined because he made the catastrophic mistake of choosing the wrong men for the job.

He'd purposely been out of town during the kidnapping to ensure that no investigators even looked in his direction, returning just in time to attend that ridiculous event last night. All that ended up doing was delaying the after effects of his men's screwup. They'd hidden his nemesis away to wait until the intense search calmed and it allowed him enough time to escape somehow. Had they really bound him as they swore they did? If so, how did he escape? He should have had him killed at once, public scrutiny be damned. The bursting need to taunt him in person, face to face, before his death had been his undoing.

He prided himself on keeping a cool head, absolutely essential when his plans had fallen through, devastating him. Given a little time, though, he'd come up with an even more satisfying plan of attack. He could think of a lot of different ways that Gideon Hale could die.

Chapter Five

Brook and Neil showed up for the Monday morning briefing at work, mugs of hot coffee in hand. Maybe the brew would provide some calm needed to endure their boss's long-winded meetings. At five minutes to ten, they entered the crowded conference room and found seats at the back, cringing at the feel of the hard plastic chairs that had surely been chosen to keep them uncomfortable. Their less than satisfactory boss, Special Agent In Charge Alan Holstein, stood at the front of the utilitarian room, struggling to look as if he belonged there. The agents, praying his bumbling leadership wouldn't become a long-term torment, called him A Hole behind his back. Although nicknames weren't unusual in their line of work, this one was unusually harsh. She'd feel bad about that if he wasn't such an arrogant ass.

He had ascended to the position by virtue of connections rather than any noticeable leadership skills after their beloved former boss had been forced to take early retirement because of his failing health. Holstein had no street credentials to brag about because he had spent his entire career behind a desk and his lack of command experience showed up on a daily basis. Other than a few random butt-kissers, the agents jeered at his leadership style, which was to claim credit for everything himself while giving them little guidance or support. He didn't have much use for female agents, either. Although that was hardly unusual in the alphabet agencies, it still frustrated the female agents. It made such a change from their previous beloved leader, who had looked out for, and appreciated, any capable agent, regardless of sex.

"Settle down," Holstein muttered, tapping a pen into the palm of his hand, like a teacher reprimanding rebellious students. He stood, standing rigid and erect, as if by doing so he could stretch to more than his height of five-foot-eight. When the agents quieted, he resumed speaking. "As most of you know, Gideon Hale and his sister have settled back into a somewhat normal life, seemingly without any lasting repercussions. There is a growing concern, however, that Ethan Ames might try again. Although we have not revealed the identity of our suspect to him, Mr. Hale has been informed about the main components of our case. He is concerned his sister might be seen to have a similar lifestyle to those of the missing women." When a rumble of conversation started in the crowd, he waited for it to fade away before continuing. "Although she is not a career woman, she is affluent and very active in the community. Because of his experience, he is worried she might be the next target and has asked for our assistance to ensure her safety."

"What about the local police? Wasn't Lieutenant Parker handling the family?" Neil asked.

"Lieutenant Parker will still act as liaison as the case moves forward, but his department doesn't have the manpower to handle twenty-four-hour protection." Holstein smiled, his perfect caps glinting under the lights. "Because Mr. Hale is a highly regarded community leader, it's important we keep everyone content by fulfilling his requests."

The murmurs in the room grew in volume. He shushed the agents, annoyance creating lines on his face. "He has requested the team who rescued him take care of their needs. After reviewing our options, we agreed Garsky can act as security for Hale while he's at work. McKenzie," he paused, aiming a smirk in Brook's direction. "McKenzie can act as his new girlfriend and hang out with the sister during the day. He's apparently between companions at the moment, so there's no one to be inconvenienced or upset by this charade. During the evening hours, you will likely be with Hale, McKenzie, while Garsky watches over Tess."

Wolf whistles filled the air. She ignored them and shook her head in dismay. "As much as I like Tess, that's hardly my typical job."

"Typical doesn't count until we catch this suspect, so no complaints," Holstein snapped. "Count yourself lucky. Mr. Hale said he'd buy you the requisite wardrobe and anything else you'll need. So, suck it up, princess." She wondered if he knew he could be censured for speaking to her so disrespectfully, but she maintained a stoic expression. Making a fuss over his comments wasn't worth the paperwork or the payback she was sure to suffer. *Let the little jerk play his silly games.* He'd never liked her because she was both female and taller than him.

He piled his papers together, made a neat stack, and shoved them under one arm. The gesture made her laugh. The papers were just for show—he hadn't consulted them even once. It made her wonder if most of them were blank. "Be at Mr. Hale's residence by noon. I'll expect reports twice a day, more often if anything of interest happens. The rest of your team will continue taking turns shadowing Ames and his cohorts. Now, get to work."

She and Neil let everyone else file out in front of them. Fidgeting, he ran a hand through his hair. "Of all the orders I expected from that asshole, this wasn't even on the list of possibilities."

"Imagine how I feel. I'm going to have to wear damned high heels all over the place." She moaned. "And plaster on makeup every day—my personal idea of hell."

"I've never thought of you as a rich guy's sidepiece. What a hoot." Ignoring her glare, he laughed, the rusty bass tone rumbling through the room. "Well, at least we get to hang out with your buddy. That should be fun. We've had worse assignments."

Warmth spread through her. "I wish it was for a better reason, but I guess we'll take what we can get." And catching Ames at long last would look great on their resumes.

At their respective apartments, they packed their go bags, some basics that included a few changes of clothes and spare guns with ammunition. After that, she picked Neil up at his place, so they'd only have one car to hide at the residence. Goodness knows, neither of their cars would fit in in that neighborhood. He climbed into Brook's aging brown sedan and relaxed in the passenger's seat as she headed across town. Travelling to an exclusive neighborhood a world apart from their own took forty minutes. As expected, her car looked like a poor relative of the vehicles they could see in the neighbors' yards as they located the correct property. Relieved to find that the news crews had finally disappeared, they offered their names and identification to the gruff officer at the gate. He checked them out, handed them back, and pressed the gate opener to permit their entry.

Neil had only seen the treed portion of the back of the property the other morning when he'd scouted for a place to drop off Gideon. Approaching the rambling house now, he whistled at the huge, white colonial with the wrap-around front porch and the lawn that stretched in front of it. "Looks like the damn grass was trimmed with nail scissors. There isn't a weed in sight." They pulled around the large, circular driveway and came to a stop in front of a massive four car garage. As they idled, wondering where she should park, a tall, slender man appeared out of nowhere. Like magic, the far garage door went up and he waved for them to continue inside. A small, red compact and an SUV shared their space with one bay left empty. Once parked, they climbed out of the car, shutting the doors.

The older man strode forward. He stuck out his hand, smiling, to shake their hands. "I'm Henry, Mr. Hale's house manager. He was delayed at work, unfortunately, but Tess is waiting for you in the kitchen. Please come with me."

Leaving their bags in the trunk for now, they followed the man inside and up a long hall with four or five different doors off it. One of them burst open as they neared the end. Tess popped out and slid a little on the polished wood floor in her haste. Once she skittered to a stop, she stared at them, grinning, and shrieked, "It's really you." Launching herself at Brook, she wrapped her arms around her waist, bursting into tears. Brook stood firm, hugging her, smiling over her head at Neil.

Eventually, Tess released her, wiping her eyes, and stepped back. "Oh, my goodness, I'm so sorry." She peered up at Neil, looking like a fairy standing next to a fabled giant. "You guys saved my brother."

"It's our job." Never much one for words, Neil looked smitten, his face flushed.

Tess grabbed them both by the hand. "Henry made lunch, so I hope you haven't eaten. I baked us a cake to celebrate." She hopped through the doorway, dragging them along in her wake. The massive kitchen had a vast granite island and a storage haven of gleaming wooden cupboards. An iced cake sat cradled on a crystal platter on the counter. The top of the cake read Even Steven in ornate letters. A picture of the two of them from their university days lay beside it.

Neil picked the photograph up for a closer look. "You look young and innocent," he said to Brook, chuckling. "Boy, those days are long past."

She pivoted toward her friend who stood beaming next to them. "You remembered the reference, then. I wasn't sure you would."

"I couldn't believe it when my brother told me. I almost drove him crazy babbling about the story, but I knew it had to be you."

Henry appeared through the door to rejoin them. "Let your guests take a seat, Tess, and I'll serve lunch." He waved to a big, sunny, adjacent room where four places had been set at a charming table made of a polished cherry that matched the cabinets. After a moment, he emerged from the kitchen. Carrying a big salad along with a platter full of sandwiches, he set them down before returning with several different dressings and a pottery jug filled with lemonade.

"Why don't you join us, Henry?" Their hostess waved to the fourth setting. "We can set another place for Gid."

"Thank you, but no. I'd like to finish getting the guest bedrooms arranged." Backing away, he added, "Mr. Hale should be home shortly. Enjoy your lunch." With that, he disappeared through the doorway.

She lifted the platter, helped herself to a few dainty sandwich triangles, and passed it to Neil. Following her example, he took a small amount, making Tess laugh. The carefree sound of it was so familiar, it made Brook grin. "Gosh, take more than that. A man your size will starve to death if you don't. Gid will take at least six or eight of them when he comes." She placed another bunch on his plate for him. Brook almost laughed aloud at his comical look of relief. "The kitchen's always open, so help yourselves. Eat as much as you want. If Henry makes something for a special purpose, he'll always put a label on it so we know."

Brook turned to peer through the back window. "This is a beautiful property. How long have you lived here?"

"Gid stumbled across this place four years ago, taking a shortcut on his way home from the office. It needed a lot of work, but after renovations we were able to move in and have it exactly how we wanted. We've been here for three years." She took a bite of her sandwich, chewed, and swallowed. "What do you think of our plan to have you move in with us?"

"Who came up with the idea?" Brook asked, feeling pretty sure it must have been her.

She shrugged. "Both of us, actually. We figured if Parker said we have to have some protection, it might as well be you two. I hope it's not too boring for you."

"We're not complaining," Neil offered. "This place

is a big step up from our apartments in every way."

"I'm glad you feel that way. We want you to be comfortable while you're here." Tess took a bite and continued after she'd swallowed. "Besides us, there's Henry, who takes great care of us. Then there's Molly, who handles the housework. Henry lives here with us. Molly works during the day, but we almost never see her. She's like a cleaning godmother, but she stays out of our way and tries to get most things tidied up when we're out of the house."

"Who prepares the meals?" She gestured toward the kitchen. "It's a pretty nice setup for someone who enjoys that kind of thing."

"Henry takes care of all the meals during the week. On the weekends, Gid usually cooks and I bake. We've done it that way for years."

Brook was surprised that a man of Gideon's financial standing would spend any of his time preparing meals. As if the very thought had summoned him, the sound of a door closing led to footsteps along the hall. Gideon appeared in the doorway. He looked as if he'd stepped out of a magazine for affluent professionals, his dark, expensive suit fitting him as if he'd been born in it. "Sorry I'm late."

Neil jumped to his feet and stuck out his hand. "Mr. Hale."

He set down his coat and briefcase on an extra chair before reciprocating. "Call me Gideon. We're very informal here at home. Although I guess in public you should do the Mr. Hale bit if you're supposed to be my security."

"Yes, of course."

His gaze moved to Brook. "So, you're the infamous

Brook. I know we've met before, but I hope you'll forgive me if I don't remember many of the details."

She smiled. "I'd be surprised if you did."

Waving for them all to sit, he joined them. "I have to say, this is a rather unusual situation for me. Well, for all of us, I suppose." He loosened his tie and grabbed a sandwich. "In order for you to be effective in your roles, we decided it made more sense for you both to be part of the household."

"I agree." She liked the way he treated Tess as if he adored her.

As he chewed, he slid off his suit jacket and hung it on the back of a chair. After that, he sat once more. "Tess arranged for a wide selection of clothing from her favorite store to be brought here tomorrow morning. Please choose whatever you think appropriate for your job in your role as my companion. My work dictates a certain level of formality in my social life." He grimaced. "It's necessity, you understand, rather than choice. Tess and I are homebodies when we have the option. We prefer to eat here at the house when possible, but social obligations are a necessary evil in my business."

"I understand." She found it surprising that their attitudes about social engagements aligned.

"Oh, I forgot to ask you," Tess cut in. "Do you two like dogs?"

They both nodded. Tess jumped up and opened a door off to the side, allowing a black Labrador retriever to enter. "This is Abe." The excited dog ran to first Brook and then Neil, wiggling and wagging his tail like a flag fluttering in the wind. After he visited with everyone, he settled on a dog bed in the corner, closing his eyes.

They finished their delicious lunch in short order.

Afterwards, Gideon got to his feet, grabbing his suit jacket and briefcase. "I'm going to let Tess show you to your bedrooms. Please let me know if there's anything you require that hasn't already been provided. After I change into comfortable clothes, Neil, I'll come and find you. We can discuss my work habits, schedule, and such."

"That's a good idea."

After retrieving their things from the trunk of Brook's car, the two of them trudged up the grand staircase, lugging their bags as they followed Tess. They headed to Brook's bedroom first. Roomy and filled with light, it boasted a queen size bed with a spacious bathroom attached. Gleaming cherry antique furniture filled the space. "This is beautiful." She stopped to admire the impressionist paintings that hung on two walls.

"Nothing but the best for you." Tess grinned. "Gid's room is across the hall, but Neil and I are down the other end. Let me show him where to go, so he can settle in. I'll be back." She tugged on Neil's shirtsleeve like a little kid would and the two of them disappeared back through the doorway.

So, this is what it means to have a lot of money plus good taste. She ran a hand over the gleaming dresser. Her uncle's home where she'd been raised had been more like a museum, but this was a beautiful home at its most comfortable. The entire house had a welcoming feel which would make their transition easier.

Hanging the few clothes she'd brought with her in the closet, she tucked her underthings into the top drawer of the spacious dresser. She put her case away in a bottom corner underneath the hanging clothes. Tess reappeared and plopped down on the bed, to tuck her legs underneath her. "Neil and Gid are yakking it up in the office. Let me show you around." They strolled from one end of the home to the other, peeking through doors as she chattered. The rambling house had six spacious bedrooms, an office, two living areas, and a huge, formal dining room. "We almost never use it, though, except at Christmas and Thanksgiving," her friend commented. "If we have guests, we usually take them out to a nice restaurant instead." She finished off the tour by gesturing down the final hall next to the garage. "This is Henry's domain. We try to give him his privacy. He's earned it."

A few hours later, Henry prepared a delicious Italian dinner for them: lasagna with crusty bread and a tossed salad. Brook realized that, if she wasn't careful, she would gain pounds she didn't need while she stayed here. She and Tess spent the evening telling the guys their favorite stories from university. For better or worse, they weren't particularly scandalous, just typical shenanigans for two young women experiencing newfound freedom. Before they knew it, the clock struck eleven and they retired to their respective bedrooms.

Comfortable surroundings aside, try as she might, Brook couldn't sleep. After forty-five minutes of tossing and turning, she gave up and slipped downstairs for a glass of orange juice. She'd sat there, sipping her drink and thinking, for ten minutes when she heard a creak on the stairs, followed by a looming shadow at the door. Even in the dim light, she recognized Gideon. "I hope I didn't wake you."

"You didn't. I'm afraid I haven't been sleeping very soundly these days. Part of me seems stuck in defense mode, listening every time the wind shifts." He moved into the room, switching on one of the smaller lights. "I hope you find your room comfortable."

"It's lovely. I was a little restless and hoped a drink of juice might settle me."

He took a glass out of the cupboard and sat on the kitchen chair opposite her. "I know this is an awkward situation for both of you, but I appreciate you being here. I believed Tess would relax more if it was you and Neil here rather than total strangers. She's suspicious of almost everyone right now."

"I'm glad we can help. I would do anything for her. Besides Neil, she's the closest thing I have to family."

He chuckled. "She told me she thought Neil was 'sweet.' Not a word I would have used for someone that size in your line of work. At least she feels comfortable with him or as close as she can be under these circumstances." Reaching across the table, he grabbed the jug of orange juice she'd left there and poured himself a drink. "She tries to put a brave face on it, but she's very worried about the suspect making another attempt at snatching one of us."

"That seems like a reasonable fear given the circumstances, but that's what we're here to prevent. I'll try to find ways to reassure her."

He swallowed, pausing to meet her gaze, his cobalt eyes mesmerizing. "It's Ethan Ames, isn't it?"

Her first instinct was to deny it, but she didn't think she could fool him. She sighed, not really surprised at the accuracy of his guess. "Yes. Does Tess know?"

"No. I don't want to upset her. She's been through enough."

"I'm surprised you narrowed it down so quickly. How did you figure it out?"

Shrugging, he said, "Process of elimination, really. He's the only one who has been inordinately interested in my business in recent months. Not directly, of course, but word got back to me that he's been asking about my current interests. I'm sure that's in order to try and steal deals out from under me." He shook his head. "If he's really behind all of these crimes, it's such a shock. I knew his father. He was an honorable man as well as a reputable businessman."

"Ethan's a bad seed, I guess. It happens more often than you think. There are an estimated fifty serial killers on the loose in this country alone at any one time. Sadly, many of them never get captured."

"That's a shocking statistic." He paused to take a drink. "I had no idea the number was that high. How is it I've never heard about any of these women disappearing? When was the last body found?" He stood up again and rummaged in a ceramic jar, removing a handful of cookies. Grabbing a napkin to put them on, he set them in the center of the table so they both could reach them.

"There's a reason why you've never heard anything about these cases. The women were from five different states and no bodies have ever been found. Two years after the first two victims disappeared, we discovered a connection between the cases. A great deal of footwork finally exposed a link to Ames. He has either dated or tried to date all of the victims."

He frowned. "If no bodies have been found, why do you assume they're dead? Couldn't he be holding them prisoner somewhere?"

"Too much time has passed. There were certain items found at the scenes of their disappearances that make their deaths probable. We all pray for the time victims are found alive, but, in cases like this, it rarely happens." She took a bite, chewed, and swallowed. "Please don't tell Tess it's Ames. That knowledge would change her behavior. She's easy to read and we can't afford for him to get suspicious. With his money, he could easily disappear to some place with no extradition."

"I won't say a word because, you're right, it would make things worse for Tess. She'd be too scared to let me set foot outside the house, never mind go herself. She's already struggling with the situation as it is." They ate in silence for a few minutes before he changed the subject. "I have a business dinner tomorrow night with a client from Paris. Tess tells me you speak French."

"Yes."

"That will be helpful. My talent for other languages is non-existent, I'm afraid." He brushed off his hands and stood. "The occasion will require cocktail attire. You'll have plenty of dresses to choose from when the personal shopper shows up in the morning."

"Thank you. That's very generous."

"It's my pleasure. Besides, I'm the reason you have to carry out this charade. I'll provide you with a schedule of my social obligations before she arrives so you have an idea of how many outfits you'll require. Tess loves fashion and shopping, so she'll be excited to help." He placed the jug of orange juice back in the refrigerator and turned back toward her. "I am not given to public displays of affection, but, since you are supposed to be my lover, a certain amount of physical contact will be expected. I hope that won't make you uncomfortable."

His formal, but thoughtful, words made her smile.

"I appreciate your concern, but it won't be a problem. And I'll do what I can to make it less awkward for you." Standing, she followed him out into the hall, then up the stairs where they parted ways.

Even with the snack to settle her stomach, it took her a long while to get to sleep. Gideon had proven himself to be unexpectedly humble. Did he ever look in the mirror? As far as she could see, he was rich, handsome, and clever, not to mention thoughtful. It would be no hardship to act as his lover. It might be a bigger problem to keep her mind on her job and not get distracted. How did a man like him stay single this long? Pondering that question finally helped lull her to sleep.

Chapter Six

Brook woke the next morning to the pleasant sound of birds chirping outside her window. Surprised to see the crystal clock on the dresser read eight o'clock, she rose and headed for the bathroom. Getting to sleep in was a rare luxury. A quick shower in that heavenly, marble-clad bathroom and donning fresh clothes got her started on the day. She wandered down to the kitchen to find Tess talking to the dog. "Good morning."

"Morning, sleepyhead." She jumped up and hugged her. "The guys blew out of here a few minutes ago. Good thing, because Amy will be here with scads of glorious fashion goodies at ten. Men have no place in a shopping experience. Not if we want to have fun."

"That's true. Shopping is Neil's idea of torture." She stretched her arms above her head. "I can't believe I slept until eight. Sorry."

"Sorry for what? I was just hangin' out with Abe anyway." Tess gestured at the cereal on the table. "I eat that, but we have pretty much every kind of breakfast food."

"I usually just have coffee."

"That worked in college, but you'll need more gas in your tank today. Serious shopping takes energy." She hopped up, went to the corner cupboard, and pulled out a glass storage container which she opened with a dramatic wave of her hand. "Croissants. They're Henry's

59

specialty." Without waiting for a response, she put two on a plate and set them on the table. They looked like pieces of art, the flaky layers enticing.

"You sold me." Brook took one and bit into it, groaning with pleasure. "Oh, these are amazing."

"He baked them fresh this morning." Tess sniffed. "You can still smell them. I'm surprised the aroma didn't wake you up." Sitting down, she smiled. "I'm so happy you're here. I keep pinching myself to make sure I'm not dreaming."

"Me, too." Chewing a bite, she swallowed. "I need your help with something. If I'm going to be successful in acting as your brother's companion, you'd better tell me a little more about him. I know next to nothing about his life other than his professional success."

"There are tons of magazine articles about him, but I'm happy to spill the beans on personal stuff. He considers that off limits to reporters. What kind of information do you need?"

"His likes and dislikes. Work habits. Ex-girlfriends. Favorite and least favorite foods. Enough details to sound credible if anyone asks a question."

"Mmmm…" She tucked one foot underneath her. "He's pretty easygoing on the whole, but he's a stickler on manners. Rude people are ignored or, in extreme situations, called out." She snickered. "He broke up with his last girlfriend because she threw a drink on their waitress."

Brook tried to envision an adult doing such a ridiculous thing. "Are you serious?"

She nodded.

"Why on earth would she do that?"

"I guess the server used a cheap vodka for her drink

instead of the fancy kind. Her highness thinks she's some kind of expert on the stuff." She shrugged. "I guess when Gid objected, she told him she was just expressing her disapproval."

"Good Lord. How embarrassing for him."

Shrugging, she said, "I couldn't stand her from the start so I was thrilled when that happened and he kicked her to the curb. Her name is Amelia Barnes. She's a trial lawyer who's still trying to lure him back." Leaning down to pat Abe, she continued. "He loves dogs and horses, but he's not crazy about cats. He says they always look like they're plotting revenge."

"He's got a point."

She giggled. "He doesn't like oysters or liver and he won't eat cheap cuts of beef. They're too fatty."

"He looks like he's in good shape. Is he a health nut?"

"Nope. Thank goodness. Actually, he has quite a sweet tooth, but he works out on his lunch hour to make up for it."

"At a gym?"

She shook her head. "He hates gyms. He has a treadmill and some weights in a little room attached to his office. He usually uses his lunch hour to work out and catch up on his phone calls."

"Does he keep regular nine-to-five hours at his office?"

"More like eight to six with an evening obligation once or twice a week. He answers calls and emails on the drive in, then attends meetings most days. A lot of the biggest deals come together over a nice dinner out."

"What is his educational background?"

Abe came wandering over to try and mooch a treat.

She waved him away with a chastising fake growl. "He has a Bachelor's degree in finance and a Masters of Business Administration specializing in international finance."

"No wonder you're so proud of him."

Tears appeared at the corners of her eyes. "He's the best brother ever created. I almost lost my mind when those monsters took him. I mean it. I got hysterical." Taking a long breath in and letting it out, she repeated the story.

"I'm so glad we were there to help."

"I owe you guys everything. I honestly don't know how I could live without him." She sniffed. "I do have one question, though. How on earth did you carry him out of that horrible place? He's not little, like me."

Brook grinned, feeling compelled to cheer her up. "Like a big old bag of laundry. I left him trussed up, dragged him to the window and hoisted him over the ledge. After that, I lowered him by rope to Neil, who was waiting below."

"Oh, my gosh. I tried to visualize how you did it, but it all seemed so impossible to me."

"Believe me, it's better for him he wasn't awake. Getting carted around like dirty clothes would be too hard on his masculine pride." Their snickers were interrupted by the peal of the doorbell. They listened to Henry answering it, the sound of a woman's voice responding.

"That's Amy." Tess gestured for her to join the other woman in the vestibule. "We're restricting visitors right now, but she gets a free pass today."

Whatever Brook was expecting, it didn't include a long, packed, rolling rack of clothes being wheeled across the tile floor of the entry. A pert, female face poked out from behind, framed by a smooth blonde chignon and chic black glasses. "I'm all ready to go, Miss Hale. Do you want to use the spare bedroom like last time?"

"Yes, please." Henry led the way down the hall to the first doorway. Once he opened the door, she could see that this bedroom had a large open space beside the bed. Amy maneuvered the rack to a position against one wall and turned to them with a smile. Brook wondered if she was a size two. She looked even smaller than Tess.

Henry took a step back to stay out of the way, removing a folded sheet of paper from his shirt pocket which he handed to Brook. "Gideon left this for you. I'll leave you ladies to your fun. Call out if you need anything."

She opened the note and saw the social schedule Gideon had promised her. Huffing out a breath, she saw seven or eight events in the next month that would require cocktail or evening dresses. She showed Tess, who hummed, tapping her foot. "So, eight dresses and a few less formal outfits should be enough to get us started. Plus accessories, of course."

Just the thought of the expense made her uneasy and her practical nature intervened. "Surely, we could double up and use some dresses for more than one occasion. I'm certain it won't matter."

She gave a mocking look of horror. "Absolutely not. Gideon made that clear before he left. Only the best for his new lady love. Besides, with some of these people wearing a dress twice is a dreadful scandal."

Brook remembered the part she had to play and wondered how discreet the shopper might be. "Well, since he insisted, I guess it's time to have some fun." She watched in amazement as Amy showed her the first possibility, a stunning silver gown likely worth six months of her salary. She glanced at Tess, who wiggled past the saleswoman, grabbing another choice off the rack. "No, I think this color is more you."

It was a gleaming antique gold color, a sleeveless design. The dress had a Grecian collar, and the fitted body would show her curves. "It's stunning," she said and reached out to take the hanger.

Her friend gestured to the other side of the bed. "Try it on over there and I'll keep hunting while you change." Rubbing her hands together with glee, she headed back to the rack.

Brook took off her outer clothes, relieved that she had remembered to wear her best bra and panties. As she slid the beautiful dress on, carefully, she could hear Tess considering some and rejecting others. It was a good thing she had her friend to advise her. She never paid much attention to fashion. Sex appeal worked against you in her line of work. Four boxy suits that all looked the same took care of her work needs. She smoothed the garment over her figure carefully, loving the feel of the fine material sliding against her skin. "Can you zip me up?" Amy hurried over and did so, telling her to let them take a look.

The other two gasped, saying an, "Oh, yes," in unison as if they'd practiced it. Their synched enthusiastic reaction made her chuckle.

She turned to peer into the full-length mirror that hung on the nearest wall. Another person stared back; an elegant, more sophisticated woman than expected.

"I knew it!" Tess raised a fist in triumph, adding a

booty dance for emphasis. "It's perfect for tonight. Classy and just sexy enough without going overboard. Let's keep going."

It took an exhausting two hours trying on clothes and experimenting with accessories, but, in the end, she'd gathered everything she needed for the foreseeable future. The assortment of clothes lying on the bed was more than she'd purchased in the last five years. Tess wouldn't let her see the total bill. The enormous cost would have stopped her heart to be sure, but Gideon had said not to worry. Amy looked delighted when she left. *Probably works on commission, so who can blame her.*

They enjoyed a lovely lunch in the stunning, white gazebo in the garden which was apparently Henry's hobby. Lush flowers in vibrant colors bloomed from every corner of the yard, their scents beckoning. "Gid and I have black thumbs, so Henry won't let us touch anything."

"I know what you mean. I always over-water plants or let them dry into dust, depending on whether we're at home or away on a case." She laughed. "You know who's great with anything that grows? Neil. He should have been a landscaper."

"Really?" She pushed her plate aside. "He's such an interesting guy. I mean, he looks like this big, tough dude, but he's really sweet. Did you guys meet at work?"

"Yes. We went through training together."

"Were you always partners?"

"I wish. No, we suffered other partners for a while, but we were finally paired together on a case. We worked together well from the start. I had a great boss and when he asked each of us who our ideal partner would be, we picked each other. That was that."

"So, you've always been no more than friends?"

She thought there appeared to be more than a normal level of interest in her question. "That's right. The best of friends, from day one. I think it's an orphan-bonding kind of thing."

"Neil has no family?"

"No. Just me."

They spent the remainder of the day chatting, with Tess doing the lion's share. It was fun to listen to her babble away—just like old times. When her questions moved to the kidnapping case, Brook made generic comments, then changed the subject back to something happier. Before long, it was time for her to get ready for her first evening out with Gideon.

Chapter Seven

Gideon had been so busy all day he didn't have much chance to think about tonight's business dinner. One glance at Brook coming down the stairs yanked his focus back into place. The clutch of attraction he felt at the sight of her caught him off guard. "Good evening." He moved forward as she arrived on the bottom step.

She smiled in response. For a moment, he wished he had a better camera than his cellphone to capture her gorgeous face. The gold dress fit her like a custom piece, accentuating her curves in a tasteful way. If he'd asked a genie to conjure the perfect companion for the night, he couldn't have done any better.

"Doesn't she look amazing?" Tess commented, from the other side of the room.

"Yes. She looks lovely." He handed her the wrap Tess had provided and helped slide it over her shoulders. "I assume the clothing Amy provided offered you with enough of a selection?"

"More than enough, thank you." They bid the others goodnight and made their way outside to the waiting car. He handed her into the passenger seat, then went around and climbed in on the other side.

"No driver?" she asked.

He started the car and left the driveway. "I hope you're not disappointed. I usually use my driver during the day, so that I can get some work done on the commute. I drive myself at night."

"Disappointed? No, you have to remember, I'm not used to having a staff take care of me. It takes some getting used to. I grew up in an affluent household, but many years of a middle-class life have passed since then."

He nodded. "At least the food tonight will be excellent and most of the company interesting. I feel compelled to warn you that one of the guests, the primary's brother, is a bit…forward when it comes to women. That's as tactful as I can be, given his typical behavior."

She met his gaze. "I'm well-accustomed to putting men gently in their place. Don't worry. I won't break his knuckles as tempting as that might be."

"I don't want you to feel insulted by his behavior. I find him rather crass, but perhaps it won't bother you. I'm a little sensitive because he's acted that way around Tess a time or two."

"Men like that are more common than you might think, especially with a job like mine. Under normal circumstances, it can be an attempt to put me in my place. Tonight, I'll just ignore him and concentrate on the other guests, but I appreciate your concern."

"I want you to be comfortable." With her reassurance, he moved on. "On my lunch hour, I read the fictitious background provided for you by your superior. It's rather frivolous compared to the real you."

She nodded. "Thank you. Did it keep you occupied while you did your workout?"

"Yes. And I shouldn't be surprised to hear that my sister's been talking about me. She confessed you'd had a chat about me when I got home from work." His eyes glittered with humor. "Should I be concerned?"

"Not really. She didn't tell me anything too provocative when I asked for details. She gave me enough information to keep our interactions a little more natural. Since we supposedly haven't been dating long, people won't expect me to know every single thing about you."

"And yet, in quite scandalous fashion, you're already living in my home. That fact alone is certain to raise a few eyebrows."

"Oh, yes. I'm sure it will be cause for some gossip." She felt a little nosy by asking, but she should probably know the answer in case it came up. "Has that ever happened before?"

He was silent for a moment and she had enough time to wonder if she'd offended him before he replied. "No. I'm actually a very private man by nature. I can hardly call myself a saint, at my age, but I'm also not given to casual affairs."

His frankness continued to both surprise and impress her. "Well, in this day and age, I'd say that's an intelligent choice."

"Because I'm not casual about affairs, and that's a well-known fact, you might be in for more scrutiny than normal. It's bound to cause some comments from others, I'm afraid. Especially other women."

Wondering if he was referring to his ex-girlfriend, she replied, "Don't worry. This job is frequently about playing a convincing role. I've become quite proficient at it over the years."

"I'm certain that will help. I wouldn't want anything to make you feel uncomfortable." He went on to tell her a little about their dinner companions and that filled the time until their arrival. The moment he stopped the car under the roof at the entrance, one valet scrambled to stand by his door and another by hers. He hurried around to her side, thanking them and handing over the keys.

The five-star restaurant was encased in a tower of modern metal and glass, typical of the finer downtown buildings. After entering the stylish lobby, all gleaming floors and modern chandeliers, they proceeded to a back elevator which whisked them to the top floor. With just one glance around, Brook had a fleeting realization that she couldn't have afforded a glass of water here.

They were met by the maître d' who did everything but kiss Gideon's hand. After a moment, an elegant blonde hostess dressed in a chic black dress and towering heels replaced the fawning man. She led them to a lovely, large table which offered a panoramic view of the downtown skyline. The other guests appeared to have already arrived. Five men and two women were introduced by a slender, gray-haired man in his sixties who raised her hand to his lips. "*Enchante, mademoiselle.*"

Whether Antoine Ferrat was really enchanted to meet her or not, it made for a lovely greeting. "*Bonsoir, monsieur,*" she answered, wishing him good evening in return.

He turned to Gideon and shook his hand while speaking to the others. "Gideon's French is a little rusty, so we will stick with English, yes?" He waved him away so he could hold Brook's chair as she sat. She identified the lecherous brother, Henri, simply by the fact that his gaze never seemed to elevate above any of the women's chests when he spoke to them. His perfectly tanned skin, overdyed ebony hair, and pudgy waistline spoke of an indolent life.

"You must tell us more about your elegant lover, Gideon. She is delicious." His body-scanning regard nauseated her, but she ignored him and pretended to be captivated by one of the other women's dresses.

She watched in her peripheral vision as Antoine shot him a quelling look and changed the subject. Brook remained quiet through the conversation, pausing every now and then to smile at Gideon or touch his hand. Antoine's wife, Elyse, proved to be quite delightful and had interesting stories to tell about their many adventures around the world. The beautifully presented food tasted delicious. With so many courses, it was lucky the servings were small. Her dress didn't allow enough room to stuff herself even if she felt so inclined.

At one point during dinner, Brook noticed that Gideon looked uncomfortable. His smiling expression suddenly seeming forced. He continued talking, but she read strain on his face and wondered what caused it. A slight shift in her chair allowed her a better angle with which to investigate. She realized, with shock, that the nervy woman seated on his other side had her hand high on his thigh in a rather intimate position. Deciding to intervene and save him, she said, "I'm so sorry to interrupt, everyone, but I'm getting a small chill from the door." She met his gaze. "Darling, would you be kind enough to switch places with me?"

"Of course," he answered, standing to help pull back her chair. When they had switched positions, he asked, "Would you like the hostess to get your wrap?"

"No, thank you." Leaning in to kiss his cheek, she added, "I'm fine, now." He squeezed her fingers in response. She ignored the woman next to her whose thwarted plans left her sulking, her glistening ruby lips thrust out in a pout more suitable to a two-year-old. *Spend a little less money on your breasts and invest more in lessons on proper etiquette.* The sarcastic thought made her smile. Her reward for switching positions was seeing Gideon relax once again and enjoy himself.

The remainder of the excellent meal proceeded smoothly with an amazing chocolate mousse as their final reward. Unable to resist such temptation, both she and Gideon ate every last spoonful. All of the guests were standing to leave, waiting for their outer wear, when Ethan Ames entered the restaurant, a towering blonde who Brook recognized as an international model at his side. She saw him wave off their hostess as he veered in their direction, leaving the model to follow, a peeved frown on her face. "Well, Gideon, this is a surprise," he said with a mocking smile, staring past him to Brook. Gideon's face expressionless, he introduced Ethan to the others, leaving her to the last. "So, this is your mystery woman." Their nemesis took her hand and stroked it, causing the model to purse her lips. "And where have you been hiding this delightful creature?"

She pulled her hand away, wishing she could scrub it with bleach. "We prefer to spend most of our evenings at home," she said with a coy smile. Curling her arm around Gideon's, she met his gaze, smiling. "Don't we, darling?"

"Absolutely." He brushed his fingertips against her lips. Turning, he thanked his host and bade everyone good evening. Once downstairs, he paid the parking stub and added a generous tip, staying silent until both were safely ensconced in the car. "Well, that was interesting," he said as they pulled into heavy traffic.

"Which part?" she asked. "The part where I had to save your purity from an over-stimulated dinner mate?"

He laughed. "Yes, thanks for that. Her antics were getting awkward to say the least. She's Antoine's niece and they adore her. Whether anyone else does is a subject for debate." Sighing, he shook his head. "I had no idea she was going to be there tonight. Her behavior, like her father's, is always questionable. She learned it from him, I guess." He paused as they turned onto a quieter street. "But, on a more serious note, I did not appreciate the way Ethan leered at you."

"Neither did his date." She said it with a smile, trying to make light of the other man's inappropriate behavior. As a woman, one had to learn how to deal with lascivious men.

His eyes darkened. "I'm serious."

"I know you are. I appreciate your concern, but the truth is it might be the best thing for everyone involved if he makes a play for me. I can handle him."

"No. I don't want you put in that position."

She noted his determined tone, but felt compelled to be honest with him. "I know you're used to being in charge, but you may not have any say in the matter. None of us do. It comes down to whatever form of enticement works to nail him to the wall."

He remained silent for a few minutes, intensity showing in the firm line of his jaw. "Is that part of the plan? To have you become the bait that might catch him?"

"It's one of the possibilities in this scenario, yes." She was the soul of practicality. No point in lying to him or insulting his intelligence. Again, the silence from the other side of the car unnerved her. She gave him a few moments to process, then spoke again. "This is what I'm trained for, Gideon. I'm not soft and gentle like Tess. I'm well-trained to protect both myself and others." She realized with a start, that they were already pulling into the driveway. She'd been too distracted to notice their progress. They entered the shadowed garage and she relaxed as the light blinked on overhead. When he shut off the car, she undid her belt and climbed out.

He was around the hood and at her side in an instant. Without pause, he put one hand on either side of her face and kissed her. The slow, searching heat of it had her moving into his arms in response. Afterwards, she stepped back, moving a finger to stroke his cheek. "We're all going to be okay," she said. "I promise we'll get through this." *But that kiss certainly complicates things.*

"You can't be certain of that." They walked down the path to the house and let themselves in the back door.

"Nothing in life is certain," she murmured. "We're both old enough to know that. Life is a gamble at best." Making their way up the stairs, they parted at their respective doors, carrying that sobering reminder with them.

Chapter Eight

A tense hour later, Gideon still lay staring at the ceiling, his thoughts stuck on the complexities of their situation. He'd landed over his head with this unusual set of problems and he didn't know how to respond to the threats they all faced. Feeling out of control frustrated him. He was used to being the one in charge. Having others make the decisions about something so important proved more difficult than he had imagined. Others might think him a little stuffy, but he'd always been a conservative man by nature, not comfortable with taking unnecessary chances in either his work or his personal life. And yet...

He had to admit he had an additional, more personal, motive for capturing Brook under his roof. She intrigued him in a way no other woman had in years. He couldn't stop thinking about her, as if that simple touch before his rescue had branded him for life. But falling for someone who spent her life practicing subterfuge seemed like a risky endeavor at best. He never took risks in anything other than business and, in that arena, he had a lot of education and experience to back him up. She kissed him back, though, and her responsiveness seemed not only genuine, but passionate. Did she feel like she had to? Or was she trying to get him to stop worrying?

Why couldn't it be simple, this sense of connection between the two of them? Or would it be less intense?

Gideon had no way of knowing. He stood alone in unfamiliar territory. It was his last thought before sleep finally came.

****

Brook rose early after a restless night and found Tess sipping coffee in the kitchen. "Morning," she said, heading for the refrigerator and snatching an empty glass out of the cupboard on the way. She took note of the early sun peeking through the curtained windows, casting lacy shadows on the far wall.

"I expected you to sleep in after being out late. How did the dinner go?"

"It was interesting. The food tasted delicious." She filled her glass with milk and shut the door, slouching into the nearest seat. Curious about her friend's reaction, she related the story about the young woman making an inappropriate approach to Gideon.

She slapped a hand over her eyes, groaning. "Oh, no. Poor Gid. Women crawling all over him always makes him so uncomfortable. It happens more often than you might think."

"And why am I poor this morning?" The subject of their conversation entered the kitchen, in an immaculate gray suit and burgundy tie. Neil followed closely on his heels. Gideon raised an eyebrow, swinging in Brook's direction to meet her gaze. "Did you tell her about me getting cornered?"

She nodded. "I couldn't resist. I hope you don't mind."

"What am I missing?" Neil asked. Brook recounted the story. His eyes bugged out as his gaze settled on Gideon. "What did you do?"

"Brook was kind enough to make up an excuse so

she could change places with me. It helped me avoid what could have become a more embarrassing situation." He smiled, leaning to pick up his briefcase from the table by the door.

Tess cleared her throat, giving her brother a pointed glare. "I know you don't eat breakfast, but that doesn't mean others don't like to indulge. Neil probably starved yesterday. I bet you didn't even notice."

A frown spread across his face and he sighed. "Guilty as charged. Neil. I'm so sorry. I didn't think. I haven't eaten breakfast in years."

"No problem."

"Yes, it's a problem," Tess replied. "Just because he does without the most important meal of the day doesn't mean you have to." Leaping up to yank open a drawer, she grabbed a resealable bag, reaching into the jar and withdrawing three croissants. She placed them inside and zipped the bag shut, handing it to Neil. Grabbing a few paper napkins, she flung her arm out with dramatic flair, shoving them at him. "There you go. Problem solved. You can eat them in the car."

His face flushed as he nodded. "Thank you, Tess. I appreciate it." The men said their goodbyes and filed out the door. The outer door banged shut.

Tess waited until the sound of the car pulling away reached them, then swung around to face Brook. "I think I embarrassed Neil."

"Don't be silly. Of course, you didn't."

"His face turned red."

She told her the truth. "Neil's just not used to having anyone except me do nice things for him."

"Why not? He's wonderful."

One sweet friend liked another. That made her

happy. The upcoming weeks should prove interesting. "He grew up in foster care, bouncing from one home to another. He was always so big, people were often scared of him. Trusting other people and their motivations doesn't come easily to him." She stood up and helped herself to a croissant, returning to her chair. "In our line of work, trusting others takes a real leap of faith."

"I get it. He had no one to love him as a kid and, now, bad guys are everywhere. I want to be extra nice to him to make up for all that." She sat back down. "Can I ask you one more thing about him?"

"Of course."

"Where did he get the scar on his face?"

The memory of it made her wince. "He got it defending me. Five or six years ago, a serial killer surprised us at a crime scene. He'd hidden in the trunk of an old car on the property after it had been searched."

"Oh, my God. I would have died of fright on the spot."

"He sprang out when my back was turned. The only thing that stopped him was Neil. It was unsafe to use a gun, so he just jumped him. I couldn't stop him before he used his knife on Neil."

"Did you shoot him?"

"Yes, I finally got a clean shot, but the damage was already done."

She shivered, wrapping her arms around herself. "How many stitches?"

"Twenty-eight. I felt terrible about it. Believe it or not, it used to be much worse. The plastic surgeon did an amazing job."

"It's not a bad scar at all. I just noticed and I was curious. Is he sensitive about it?"

"He was at first, but not anymore."

She was quiet for a minute or two, then she changed the subject. "So, what else happened last night? Was it a total snore fest?"

"It was okay. Most of the party were really friendly." She decided to test the waters. "We ran into Ethan Ames and his date on the way out."

She wrinkled her nose. "Yuck."

"Well, that's quite a reaction. Not your favorite person?"

Groaning, she replied, "He's…I don't know, kind of slick and slimy. He gives me the creeping crawlies."

Interesting that she has a sixth sense about him. "He had that blonde model from Sweden on his arm. What's her name…is it Ilsa? I remember her face because she's been on the front cover of almost every magazine in the country at one time or another."

She snorted with obvious derision. "That's the only kind of women he dates; models and assorted gorgeous young things, always much younger than him. It just raises the creepy factor as far as I'm concerned." Tilting her head, she gave a little smirk. "To be honest, I'm surprised he wasn't slobbering all over you."

"As you said, he's a little creepy, but, between Gideon and me, we managed to stave him off. From what you said, maybe I'm too old for him. That's fine with me."

"If he knows you are supposedly into Gid, he'll try for you, sooner or later. That's a no-brainer. He's very jealous that my brother is well-regarded in local society."

"And he isn't well-regarded?" Not much of a shock, given what they knew about him and his proclivities.

"No, not at all. Apparently, he's a terrible boss and

turnover in his companies is much higher than average. And he's not nearly as generous to local charities as Gid is. Both of those things really matter in the business world."

"And so, they should." She finished her croissant and took a sip of milk, stroking Abe when he wandered by for a good morning pat. "What's on our agenda for today?"

"Let's go shopping."

"Again? We just shopped here yesterday and I seem to remember you claiming a few items for yourself. It made me feel less greedy, at least."

"Those few little things don't count. Amy was coming anyway, so it was convenient. That's my excuse and I'm sticking to it." Tess laughed. "Henry's going to do the week's meal preparations today and Molly's cleaning floors, so we can't be underfoot. Besides, I have to find a present for Gid. His birthday's on Friday."

"How old will he be?"

"Thirty-seven. Anyway, maybe we could find something nice for him, then have a yummy lunch out. What do you think?"

"Sounds like fun. I haven't done anything like that in a long time." Had she ever taken the time to shop and have lunch with a friend? If so, it had been so long she couldn't remember.

They were ready thirty minutes later, dressed in comfortable slacks and blouses, grabbing jackets for the chilly breeze. Tess drove her fire-engine-red compact like a demon on steroids, zipping in and out of heavy traffic with ease. Brook had to put her seat all the way back to have room enough for her long legs, but it was rather fun to be chauffeured around for a change, even at warp speed.

They finally completed the drive downtown and ended up in an area sandwiched by clusters of towering buildings, shops, and restaurants. "Where on earth do you park around here?" She gestured to the long lines of parked cars by meters in every direction. It looked more like a car lot than a street.

"Luckily, not here," her friend answered. "We get to park in the garage of Gid's office building. He keeps an extra space there for whenever I need one."

"Well, that's convenient. You're spoiled, aren't you, but he gets bonus brother points."

"He knows I'm way too impatient to search for a space. And every parking lot charges a fortune. I usually walk around from this point because my favorite stores are all in this area. Is that okay with you?"

"Of course. I'm in dire need of some exercise after Henry's cooking."

A few minutes later, she turned into a huge, multi-level underground garage, stopping at the booth to beam a smile at the attendant. "Hi, Larry," she said to the slight, older man who smiled in response. "This is my friend, Brook."

"Welcome, ladies. Have a wonderful day." He pressed a button, then the red and white striped barricade raised to allow them entry. Tess eased forward past the security stand and turned right.

"Larry's been around for almost twenty years. He's a doll." She zipped up the ramp like a homing pigeon, zooming around the corners with ease.

Brook closed her eyes to keep from getting dizzy. "Do you know everyone around here?"

"Pretty much. Because they know I'm Gid's sister,

they pretty much treat me like royalty. Gotta be honest, I don't hate it." She zoomed up to the fifth level and slipped into a waiting parking spot, close to a single door. The engine was barely off when she popped out the car door. Opening her eyes to get her bearings, Brook followed suit. She had to remember to slow her long stride to match Tess's shorter one. Through the door, they took a glass-clad elevator down to street level and exited into the crisp morning air.

They enjoyed themselves as they wandered from shop to shop, going inside some, peering in windows of others, and swapping opinions about the wide choice of merchandise. In one, you'd find five-hundred-dollar handbags, in the next, souvenir T-shirts. The eclectic mix made it more interesting. There weren't many customers around yet, so it was the perfect time to wander. She even bought a scarf and a necklace while Tess purchased a few things.

Finally stopping in front of one of the better men's shops, Tess said, "Gid needs a new dressing gown and this is his favorite store. Once we find his gift, we'll move onto the fun stuff." After entering, they made their way to the back of the shop. Not surprisingly, the interior was classic elegance with blue, black, and silver décor. They had barely paused at the relevant rack when a slender, dapper man sped up to them, a practiced smile beaming.

"Miss Hale, delighted to see you this morning. How can I be of service? Are you looking for something for Mr. Hale?"

Brook smothered a smile. *So, this is what it's like to be rich. Even the sales staff knows your name.*

"Good morning, Jeffrey. Yes. I'm looking for a robe

for him. It's his birthday this week."

"I hope you will convey our best wishes." He stared at Brook, raising his eyebrows and offering a welcoming nod. "And is your companion looking for something as well?"

"Oh, this is Brook." She waved an airy hand in her direction.

"Miss Brook," he repeated, nodding.

"Brook is Gid's new girlfriend. She's came along to help me pick his gift out."

"That's an excellent idea. It's always better to have a second opinion, isn't it?" He moved toward the rack, searching through it, the hangers making a little zipping sound on the rail as he moved them aside. "Mr. Hale normally prefers a classic look. Should we consider this?" Holding out a burgundy robe in a heavy silk, he paused to display it for their approval.

"What do you think?" she asked Brook.

Elegant with a simple collar, it only had some decorative stitching as an accent. She looked closer, touching the fabric. "I like the style and fabric, but do you have this in another color?"

"Of course." He switched it for a deep navy.

Tess clapped her hands as Brook nodded. "You're right. That's a much better color for him. We'll take it."

"I'll get you a large from the back. And may I gift wrap that for you?"

"Yes, please. You'll do a better job than I would." He had the package ready in mere minutes, the elegant silver and blue wrapped box already placed in a handy cloth carryall. In a flash, they were back on the street, bag in hand. "That was easy peasy. I love that place. Shopping for men's clothing is so boring compared to shopping for women's stuff."

Brook turned to smile at her. "Where to, now?"

"See that sweets shop?" she asked, gesturing at a store with a pink-dotted canopy across the street. "We have to buy Gid a big box of chocolates, too."

"Can Neil and I buy them for him? I'd like us to have something to give him, since he's been so generous with us."

"You're so thoughtful. That would be great. Henry will make him dinner and an amazing cake, but he still loves his sweets." They crossed at the closest corner light, hurrying when a taxicab almost mowed them down. Once safely inside the shop, they cruised the aisles, investigating huge containers boasting treats of every description: hard candies, taffy, and jellybeans in every flavor and some more expensive chocolate creations. In the end, Brook broke the budget on, not only the large box of chocolates for Gideon, but lime jellybeans for Neil and a big bag of black Finnish licorice for herself.

Tess grimaced at her choice. "I can't believe you eat that stuff. It tastes like tar."

She grinned. "No, it doesn't. I tried some in Finland one time and got addicted. You should give it a chance."

"Blech," she said. "No thanks." She grabbed her arm. "All these sweets have revved my appetite. Time for lunch." Checking out, they gathered up their parcels and headed down the street, dodging other pedestrians as the sidewalks became more crowded.

On her recommendation, they ate just down the street in a charming French café with blue and white striped tablecloths. Greenery sprouted from little terracotta pots on the walls. After perusing the menu written on a chalkboard, Brook ordered a wedge of cheddar bacon quiche and fresh fruit while Tess chose a huge omelet with bacon. "I guess you can still eat a lot and never gain wait," Brook commented. "That wasn't fair when we were in school and it's certainly not fair now."

She giggled. "I know. My brother complains about it all the time, because I don't have to exercise nearly as much as he does." They ate their lunches while chatting and watching the passersby. On the way out, they paused in front of a display of tempting baked goods. Waving at all the different choices under the glass counter, Tess said, "Let's surprise him and Neil with desserts. We can drop them off at the office on our way out."

They picked a cherry turnover for Neil and a huge brownie for Gideon. Strolling back to the garage, they paused to drop their other parcels in the car trunk before continuing to the elevators which sped them upward to a huge suite of offices. An oversize reception desk sat inside the sheer glass entrance. The elegant silver-haired woman who sat there greeted them with a smile. "Hello, Tess." She paused as Tess introduced her, then Enid continued. "He's still on the treadmill, so you can go right back. I'll let him know you two are on the way."

She followed her down a long hall to the far corner where she opened a door, calling, "Surprise." Both men were inside the small room, Neil lifting some weights as Gideon stepped off the treadmill. The power purred to a stop.

"To what do we owe the honor?" he asked, wiping his face with a towel as he moved toward them. Brook forced her eyes to stay on his face and not drift to how fit he looked in the sweaty T-shirt and sweatpants that clung to his body. You'd think he'd look better in a suit than gym clothes, but he looked quite edible in both.

Tess waved the box of treats under his nose. "You don't need to quit your workout on our account. We brought you both a treat."

"I'm finished, anyway." He opened the box, gesturing to Neil who came to stand beside him. They both peered inside, making appreciative hums of approval. "Thanks. That will be worth the workout."

Enid's voice sounded from a small metal box on the wall. "Sir, Amelia Barnes is here and wondered if she might have a moment of your time."

He winced, a look of embarrassment lingering. "Give me two minutes, Enid, and then send her back to the office."

"Yes, sir."

"That's my cue to leave," Tess muttered, motioning for him to lean down so she could kiss his cheek. "Promise you won't let her throw drinks on anybody." She giggled at her brother's chastising look. "We'll see you two at dinner."

She hustled down the hall as Brook followed, slowing as they moved toward a very attractive blonde in a stylish business suit who stood near the entrance, glancing at her watch. The woman looked up in surprise as Tess said hello. "I don't believe you've met Gid's girlfriend," she said with a determined smile. "Brook, this is Amelia Barnes."

"Brooklin Holt," she said, using the fake surname she'd adopted as she inclined her head. "It's a pleasure to meet you."

The skin puckered around the other woman's lips and her eyes narrowed. She murmured, "A pleasure," then moved past them. They watched as she hurried in Gideon's direction, high heels clicking against the tile.

Bidding farewell to Enid, Brook waited until they were in the elevator, alone, before she spoke. "I have never seen you act bitchy before. It was reassuring, actually. It means you aren't perfect after all."

"Oh, come on," Tess grumbled, rolling her eyes. "Men are so clueless. She wants to be seen on his arm and scoop up some cash or attention. She's a social climber extraordinaire."

"Well, she's a lawyer. At least she's not some brainless bimbo."

"Gid can't do dummies. Seriously. But he should have seen through her act before the whole waitress incident." She chuckled. "At least he'll be stinky, since they hadn't had time to hit the showers yet. Maybe his hard-earned body odor will scare her off. We can always hope."

They exited the elevator, laughing, and climbed into her car. As they headed home, Tess continued to wreak havoc on the poor woman. "My theory is that she must have been good in bed. I think that's why he stayed as long as he did. I mean, every man has needs, am I right?"

"And every woman, hopefully," Brook offered. That kiss the previous night had stirred something in her that she'd had to smother to stay focused on their objective.

"Well, true, of course, but you know our parts are pickier than their parts, usually. At least mine are. I guess I can't speak for you."

Brook groaned. "Oh, my gosh, I've missed you. I have missed you so much."

"Then you shouldn't have left."

The curt words came as a surprise. A stab of guilt speared her and she glanced at her friend as the cars whizzed by in the background. "I'm so sorry for that. Truly. I wasn't given much choice."

She kept her eyes on the road, her smile uncommonly absent. "Couldn't you have trusted me? I would have kept your secret." Her voice trembled a little, making Brook feel even worse.

"They didn't want me to have any ties at all, if possible. When you do undercover work, they don't want anyone who will ask questions about where you've gone. It's less messy that way."

"Is that why they chose Neil? Because he was an orphan? I mean, I know he's smart enough and everything, but was it a factor?"

"It's not essential, but it's helpful in our line of work. No question about that."

"I don't mean to be rude, but it sounds like a lonely life."

"It is." She smiled. "But I always had Neil and he had me. It made everything easier."

"You mean he's sort of like your brother?"

"He is my brother in every way that counts. The best brother you could ever want. He can even tell what I'm thinking before I say a word."

Her shoulders finally relaxed. "Well, call me selfish, but I hope this case lasts forever. That way, you two can stay with us. It would make up for what I call the lost years." They stayed on less sensitive subjects the rest of the way home.

Later in the evening, when they all sat around the fire and told stories, she considered Tess's words about wishing the case would last forever. She realized that, despite all the hard work, she was beginning to feel the same way.

Chapter Nine

Ethan sat alone in his luxurious bedroom, having sent his companion home despite her whining protests. Seeing Gideon Hale at his favorite restaurant last night had spoiled his good mood. Wishing that annoying bastard away wasn't working, even after implementing what had looked like a foolproof plan. And, now, he would be on his guard with additional security traipsing around.

Time for a change of plans. He had to find out more about the gorgeous creature currently at Gideon's side. He didn't recognize her or her name, which seemed almost impossible, given his appetite for women. Tomorrow, he would have one of his peons dig up some delicious dirt on her. A striking woman like that had to have had plenty of former lovers—there had to be something in her past he could use as leverage against them both.

And, if not, surely he possessed the means to entice her in his direction. Hale was a bit of a puritan, the perennial good guy. *How bloody boring.* Watching how others virtually bowed to him sickened Ethan. How would he feel if this new conquest was revealed to be just like most other women, willing to sell their bodies to the highest bidder? A chance of having the sheer pleasure of rubbing that fact in his arrogant face couldn't be ignored.

Perhaps beautiful Brook could be seduced into

joining his select entourage. The very idea gave him the hard-on he'd been missing earlier. *What a waste.* He shouldn't have let the model go, after all. Using one woman while thinking of another was well within normal parameters for him.

If Hale was on guard, grabbing either his childish sister or his elegant new lover might be the way to gain access to him. Which one would be the more delectable? Taking Tess might destroy him, but losing his woman would keep him in constant agony. He liked that idea. *Constant agony.* The idea energized him and he retired to bed with only his deviant plans to keep him company.

****

"Do you need some help?" Tess called through the door. Why she indulged in formalities this time was a puzzle. She'd just charged in every other time.

"Absolutely." Brook slid the evening dress off the padded hanger as the door opened. Her friend came in and perched on the footboard of the bed, swinging her legs.

"Oh, I love that one."

Brook chuckled as she unzipped, then slipped into the gown. "You say that about every single piece of clothing we bought. You really are a fashionista."

"Well, that's true, I guess, but your body is made for evening wear. Tall and slender." She sighed. "Midgets like me can never get the same effect, no matter how hard we try. I'd have to wear stilts to compete."

"You're not a midget. You're petite. Quality not quantity." Turning, she stooped down a little so her friend could reach the top. "Can you zip me?"

She scurried over to do the job. When Brook swiveled to face her, she whistled with the lusty enthusiasm of a trucker. "Holy blue jeans. Gid is going to lose his mind."

"Why? What's wrong?" Brook responded, peering in the mirror. The teal green gown had a lovely shimmer, even if it was cut a little lower than she would normally wear. Well, a lot lower, actually. She'd have to be careful not to flash anyone unintentionally.

Tess started laughing. "Better watch it. The way you look tonight, Amelia's going to shove a dinner fork in your heart." She sobered, tilting her head. "You need to take your hair down, though."

"Wouldn't it look more elegant up?"

"No. Take my word for it. With this neckline, wearing it down is what you want." She leaned forward, plucking a pin from Brook's hair.

"Seriously? I just put it up."

"Yes, I know. Trust your fashion guru. Take it down."

There went thirty minutes of painstaking work. She sighed, pulling the rest of the bobby pins out. She sat when commanded to do so. Tess scooted around her with a brush and a curling iron for ten minutes, then insisted on heavier eye shadow and mascara. A final blast of hairspray finished the chore. "Now, take another look."

She turned to gaze in the mirror. The huge difference that one small change made stunned her. Looking exotic and sexy wasn't usually in her repertoire. *What the hell.*

"Wait," Tess said as they prepared to leave the bedroom. She plucked through the accessories on the dresser. "These earrings are the ones you want." Racing forward with a pair of lustrous gold drops, she motioned for her to bend down while she exchanged them for the studs Brook had chosen. "That's better. Now, you're done."

"Thanks. I guess there's a lot you could teach me about fashion." A sudden, nervous thrill crept down her back and she brushed it impatiently away, heading down the stairs to where Gideon and Neil waited together in the front hall. At the sound of the women's steps, they turned.

Neil gave a long whistle. "Who the hell abracadabra'd you?"

She laughed and continued toward them while Tess sped ahead of her. "Doesn't she look amazing?"

Gideon's gaze met hers. "She does, indeed." The timbre of his voice had her nerves jumping. He stepped forward and his fingers brushed along her arms as he helped with her coat. Attempting to ignore the zing of heat that followed, she smiled. Saying goodnight to the other two, they left and entered the waiting car.

His silence made her nervous. "Tell me about this gala tonight, so I won't make a blunder."

"This one's to raise money for art classes for underprivileged children." He pulled into the street. "A worthy cause, so it will be crowded, but the food is usually quite tasty. Afterwards, instead of the usual boring speeches, there is a live auction. It's often quite entertaining. The bids can soar if two people want the same thing."

"Will Ethan be there?"

"Oh, no doubt. He suffers from a constant need of publicity." His jaw tightened. "I'm afraid Amelia will be there as well. I realized I'd better warn you."

"And, is her attendance a good thing?"

"No, not really. I'm rather concerned that she might

be unpleasant to you. During her visit the other day, she asked if I would escort her to this event and I declined. She wasn't too pleased and that's putting it mildly."

She leaned over to pat his arm. "I'm quite good at putting bitchy women in their place. Don't worry about it."

"You shouldn't be subjected to her infantile tantrums."

"Nor should you." She met his gaze. "Let's concentrate on having a lovely time."

"That's a great idea. Because of your company, I'm looking forward to the evening."

A few minutes later, they pulled up in front of the hotel, waiting their turn in line before they left the car to the valets. On entering the lobby, she discovered a huge amount of artwork circling the perimeter, everything from modern to impressionist and onward. When they strolled over to look, she caught his hand, entwining their fingers. One colorful painting in particular caught her eye, a modern interpretation of a mountain scene, done in vibrant colors. "Do you like it?" he asked as she came to a stop to study the flowing lines.

"I do," she answered. "I don't know much about art, but it's something unexpected and different to find here in the city. And the mix of colors is so appealing. It makes me wish I was more artistic." They had barely proceeded twenty feet farther when Amelia appeared, stepping right in front of her as if she didn't exist. *Talk about getting a literal cold shoulder.*

"There you are, Gideon," she purred, one hand going up to stroke his jacket's lapel. "I've been waiting for you to make an appearance."

"Good evening, Amelia." He turned to Brook. "I

believe you know—"

"We've already met," she interrupted with a barely perceptible sneer. "The mayor wants to say hello. Why don't you let your little friend stay and look at the paintings while we pay our respects?" Turning, she beamed a triumphant smile in Brook's direction. "I'll bring him back in a few minutes."

"Actually," he pried her fingers from his tuxedo jacket and stepped back, "Brook and I will be along after we finish looking at the art. Locating Jack is never a problem. I'll just follow his entourage."

"But—"

"In a few minutes, Amelia." Fury leapt into her gaze. Thwarted, she spun on her heel and left, shoving through the crowd.

Brook slipped her arm through his own and leaned in. "You weren't kidding. She was not happy to lose you."

"She'll get over her disappointment." He lifted her hand and kissed her fingers. They continued on their way along the side of the packed lobby, stopping now and then to visit with other friends along with acquaintances. They eventually caught up with the mayor who seemed quite fond of Gideon. Joking about the milling crowd, they joined in, moving toward the doors. She ignored the stares and curious questions she heard whispered as they passed.

After picking up drinks inside at the bar along one wall, they made their way over to Gideon's reserved table which bore the name of his company on the placard leaning against the floral centerpiece. The only person she'd met at the table was Enid, the receptionist, but the others were quite welcoming and included her in their conversations. As he had promised, the food tasted delicious. After the fresh, colorful salad, salmon and a lovely filet of steak served as the entrée. Dessert was an enticing white chocolate truffle which everyone seemed to enjoy.

In the lull after dinner and before the auction, as staff cleared the tables, Ethan made an unwelcome appearance. He sauntered up behind Brook, saying, "Well, so we meet again." He ran his hands down her upper arms, giving her the wrong kind of chills and earning himself a steely look from Gideon. "Are all of you ready to spend a lot of money at the auction?"

"Of course." Gideon forced a smile. "Has anything captured your fancy?" It didn't escape her notice that his words came from between clenched teeth.

He moved around to face Brook, lifting an eyebrow. "I certainly see something that interests me. I just don't know if I can afford it."

She felt Gideon tense beside her and she touched his leg under the table in warning. "If you don't win it," she replied, turning to face their nemesis, "then perhaps you weren't meant to have it in the first place." She lifted her date's hand, stroked his one knuckle against her face and smiled up at Ethan. "Gideon and I are big believers in destiny, aren't we, darling?"

He leaned closer and played the game by sliding his arm around her shoulders. "Absolutely. It certainly worked for me."

Ethan's lips thinned and whitened. He inclined his head, saying, "Will you excuse me? I had better return to my seat. It seems all the action is about to begin." She watched him walk away and breathed a sigh of relief. Even Gideon's temper could only resist being goaded for so long.

A fun-loving auctioneer encouraged all to participate. The small, less expensive pieces came up for bid first and the spirited bidding made it enjoyable to watch. She had no idea about the value of each piece, but some of them went for high prices. Of course, some of the attendees would just consider it a charitable donation. About halfway through the sale, the mountain picture she had admired came up and, after the bidding lagged, Gideon raised his paddle.

She leaned toward him. "What are you doing?" she whispered.

"I'm buying you a picture."

"Gideon…"

"You worry too much. Remember, it's for a great cause."

She recognized the look of determination in his eyes and knew any objection would be a waste of time. As the bidding neared closing with his bid the coming winner, another bidder jumped in. They turned to find Ethan standing across the room with his paddle raised. Brook knew he was doing it just to aggravate Gideon. The bid already stood at five thousand. "Just let it go. It's not worth bidding any higher." Brook really didn't have a clue about its value. She just didn't want him to get carried away in combat with their mutual enemy.

Gideon nodded to the smooth-tongued auctioneer and Ethan immediately followed suit. She listened in mounting dismay as the bids climbed higher and higher. Other guests in the crowd began to murmur and egg on both bidders, causing a rising crescendo of noise. They recognized a duel when they saw it even though hard cash replaced pistols. She repeated her protests in his ear and, smiling, he ignored her. It was a side of him she hadn't seen before—the ruthless competitor.

She sat in stunned silence when Gideon's bid won the day at twenty-one thousand dollars. Feeling certain the painting wasn't worth nearly that much made her feel sick to her stomach. With a calm expression, he swiveled toward her, kissing her cheek. "Look happier," he whispered in her ear. "This is everyday life for this crowd."

He was right. She couldn't forget how playing her part was integral to their success. For these people, that amount equaled pocket change. Reaching over, she thanked him, stroked his cheek, and beamed. A few minutes later, he gestured toward the exit. "Shall we? I think we've both had enough excitement for one night." At her agreement, they bade everyone goodnight and headed out.

It was a relief to get out of there, away from all the curious stares. They paused at the auction desk to pay for the picture and make arrangements for its delivery the following day. She had to pretend that the enormous size of that check didn't affect her. No one had left immediately before them, so the usually busy coat check was empty except for the attendant. While they were waiting for their garments to be located, Brook spied Ethan watching them from a shadowed alcove down the hall.

She moved to stand in front of Gideon, so her back was to their observer. "Don't freak out," she murmured as she slipped her arms around his waist and kissed him. The heat with which his lips met hers was a welcome surprise as he stepped closer, running his fingers through her hair.

A moment later, the clerk cleared her throat. Brook stepped away, flushed, as Gideon grabbed her coat. He held it open for her and kissed the nape of her neck as she slid it on, the heat of contact tingling down her spine. She waited while he donned his coat. Slipping her arm through his, she moved forward and they exited, hearing other people following behind them. One quick glance told her their voyeur had disappeared.

Gideon remained silent for most of the short drive home and she couldn't read his mood. She didn't know whether he had spied Ethan standing in the dark corner or not. Should she explain her actions? He spoke up, startling her. "If you're worried about the cost of the painting, I was going to donate twenty-thousand anyway, so we'll consider your picture a bonus."

"Gideon, I—"

"That was pretty quick thinking on your part." He glanced across at her. "Standing by the coat check, I mean." *So, he had seen Ethan.*

She remained silent as he pulled the car into the driveway and around to the garage. "I have to—"

"You have to do your job. Believe me, I get it. But you are intentionally making yourself a target and nobody informed me that was part of the plan." He undid his seatbelt and, opening the door, climbed out, leaving her to follow. When she did, he continued, "Being aware of the possibility and encouraging it are two different things."

She walked around to join him, feeling compelled to respond. "Would you rather it was Tess?" The stark words echoed down the darkened drive. When he pivoted back toward her, she saw a haunting fear in his eyes, lit by the overhead light. Seeing his response, she regretted her impulsive words.

"It can't be a choice between the two of you. There has to be another way." He added nothing else as she joined him on the walk to the door. Letting themselves into the house, they walked upstairs in silence. He said goodnight, closing his door behind him. For the first time since this began, it felt like an insurmountable wall between them.

She pulled on cozy, cotton pajamas in a search for comfort and found only restlessness. An eternal hour later, she continued to fret. A report to her supervisor was due in the morning. She had good news that the bait appeared to be working, but it appeared, on a personal level, she was making a mess of this. She found Gideon attractive and felt drawn to him, but she had never realized he might feel the same way. The kiss they'd shared—nobody could fake that kind of response. They were both mature enough to recognize that.

Chapter Ten

Brook spent the night tossing and turning, waiting to rise in the morning until she finally heard Gideon's car leave. A cool shower woke her up and persuaded her sluggish body to get moving. She padded down to the kitchen in sock feet to find Henry and Tess making pancakes.

"Good morning."

"Morning, slowpoke," Tess answered, wiggling a spatula in the air. "We were going to send Abe upstairs to wake you. You can't miss Henry's pancakes. They are to die for."

The enticing aroma convinced her to indulge. When they were ready, Tess set a stack of them on the table and the three of them helped themselves. They had real maple syrup, too, not the cheap kind—the very definition of comfort food, much needed this morning. "I wish we could convince Gideon to eat breakfast," Henry said, "but good luck with that."

"He wouldn't have been so grouchy this morning if he did."

"Why? What did he say?" Brook couldn't help a flare of guilt.

Tess made a face. "Well, he never really complains about anything, but I can always tell when something's up." She finished a bite. "He gives new definition to the word, 'stoic.' " Lifting the jug of maple syrup, she dripped looping designs on her pancake. "Didn't you guys have fun last night?"

"Yes," she answered. "But he spent way too much on this painting I admired."

"Don't worry about that. Gid really likes giving people gifts. I hope Amelia noticed he bought it for you." She hadn't seen the woman after that initial tussle which she now told Tess about. Clapping her hands, she said, "Wish I could have seen that one. Serves her right."

"I must say, that woman was never one of my favorites," Henry said in his usual understated style. There was no polite way to respond, so Brook kept quiet. The rest of breakfast was eaten in silence. When she and Tess offered to help clear the dishes, he shooed them away. They headed upstairs, Brook waving her ahead. "What should we do today?"

"Do you still like horses?"

"Yes, but I haven't ridden in a couple of years."

"Doesn't matter. There's a riding group close by who gives equine therapy to people with disabilities. They always need helpers. Are you game?"

"I'd love that."

"I know the woman who owns the farm and she'll let us go for a trail ride afterwards if we want. There are always horses who need exercise." Changing into jeans, boots and T-shirts, they were on their way thirty minutes later.

They had a wonderful, exhausting day, helping with the children, then having a long ride on some picturesque trails that looped the outskirts of the sprawling farm. The work and exercise calmed Brook and allowed her to recall how much the company of her friend meant to her. Returning to the house afterwards, smelling of horses, they had showers and emerged to find the guys had arrived home.

Gideon was inspecting the auction painting which had been delivered that afternoon. Tess oohed and ahhed over the brilliant colors and Brook told her the story about him outbidding Ethan for it. "I wish I'd been there," she replied. "He deserves to lose out. He's always trying to outshine Gid, like a jealous child. What an ass."

"Those are pretty strong words coming from you."

"That awful man deserves them."

Neil cornered Brook while the other two were standing at the bar mixing drinks for everyone, concern sobering his expression. "Did you and the boss have a fight or something?"

"A little misunderstanding. Why?"

He shrugged. "He acted a little off kilter all day. Nothing major. I wondered if something was up between the two of you."

"I'll work it out with him. Don't worry." She smiled to reassure him. Neil was a born peacemaker, despite his threatening size. "What did you two do last night?"

"Watched some old movies. Ate a tub of popcorn. Nothing too crazy." He flushed and fidgeted.

She knew the telling signs. He was really attracted to her. "Let me guess…Doris Day, Rock Hudson?"

"She really likes them and she knew most of the dialogue by heart."

"I know. Some things never change. She used to say she'd make a perfect fifties housewife." They moved across the room to rejoin the others.

Later, when the other two were distracted by something on the news, she went to sit next to Gideon. "I'm sorry about our disagreement last night."

He sighed, turning to face her. "I'm the one who should be apologizing. This is an awkward situation for all of us. It's hard to know where the boundaries lie. I feel like I'm always out of my element, stumbling over them."

Understanding the perilous nature of their jobs always proved hard for civilians to understand. "Our number one priority is to protect you and Tess. Anything else has to be secondary to that objective."

His hand brushed hers. "I appreciate that, but I don't want to see anything happen to you and Neil, either."

"It won't." She would do everything in her power to keep her word, but he knew better.

"I think we both know that's an impossible promise to make."

"Maybe so, but Neil and I have a lot of training and experience to back that up. Not to mention a pristine record for surviving people like him in the past."

"I suppose that's true. I promise that, moving forward, I'll try to keep your excellent qualifications in mind."

Tess came over, gesturing. "Come on, you two. We're going to play a few hands of poker before bed. If I beat Neil, he has to go clothes shopping with me."

Needless to say, Neil found a way to avoid the dreaded threat, much to Tess's disappointment. Obviously, she hadn't quite figured out that she already had him wrapped around her finger. All she had to do was ask and he'd follow her anywhere, even to shop for clothes. Two hours later, they all split off and went to their respective rooms. Brook lay, restless, for an hour, wondering if Gideon was still awake. Decision made, she put on her dressing gown, wondering if she could hear if he was sleeping through his door. She eased hers open.

His bedroom door stood ajar. It never had before tonight. As she stood trying to decide what that might mean, his deep voice sounded from inside the walls. "I wanted you to know you would be welcome, in case you were inclined to join me."

Walking across the hall and through his doorway, sensual promise strummed through her. She found him lying on his bed with the sheets pulled back. Clad only in lounging pants, he stole her breath. His broad shoulders tapered to a fit waist and his defined chest muscles made her mouth water. For one surreal moment, they stared at each other, assessing. She finally moved, closing the door behind her. Turning to face him, she admitted, "I don't think this is going to make our unusual situation any less complicated."

"I'm afraid you're right. And yet, even my reputation for being sensible can't keep me away from you. Especially if you feel the same way."

"If I didn't, I wouldn't be here."

"Then why don't you come and join me?" She walked over to stand in front of him, slipping off her robe. His intake of breath reached her and she watched as his intense gaze scorched her skin. He stood and she undid the string of his pants, letting them fall to join her robe on the floor. She lay down on the bed, scuttling over so he could settle next to her. It had been a long time since she'd been intimate with anyone. Being unwilling to settle for less than an excellent connection often meant sexual pleasure took a back seat to everything else.

Having him touch her wasn't casual exploration. When his skin skated across hers, every nerve awakened and came leaping to life. Fatigue fled. His roaming mouth tasted her and she reciprocated, learning the lines and angles of his muscular body. There was no need to hurry, now. Their progression was an aching, ravenous voyage of discovery that changed moment to moment. Her hunger had, at long last, met its mate.

Afterwards, when they lay breathless, he stroked her hair. "I knew being with you would be like this. When you kissed me last night, I knew exactly how I would feel, lying next to you."

She couldn't help asking, "And how is that?"

"Incredible. Like I could slay dragons and conquer the world." He rolled to face her, his hand grazing her cheek. "Stay with me until morning."

"Henry—"

"Henry doesn't get up until six. So, if you're worried about appearances, you're safe until at least five-thirty."

"And Tess?"

He chuckled. "I hate to break it to you, but if Tess found out, she would probably throw a parade in our honor."

****

Ethan raised the braided leather whip as high as he could, lashing it down on the woman's bare flesh, relishing her screams. This was the best aphrodisiac of all, he mused, stroking himself with his other hand. He didn't bother to look at his current victim's face anymore. Closing his eyes, he envisioned Hale's lover lying there instead of this pale, pathetic rack of bones. Soon, when fortune smiled on him once again, he would have yet another sacrifice to take her place.

When Ethan finished, he opened his eyes, taking in the thick, steel bars that jailed her. He felt nothing but revulsion at the sight of his latest inmate. He shoved her onto the threadbare mattress, watching as she curled into a ball, sobbing. "Nobody will ever find you," he taunted. "Next time, you'd better scream harder or I might decide I've had enough of you. You can join your predecessors in eternal silence where you belong." She'd once been the stunning only daughter of a society family who had shunned him. They had lived to regret their arrogance, as had she.

He buttoned and zipped his clothes before leaving, slamming the door shut and locking it behind him. The clanging sound bothered his sensitive ears. A male attendant, thin, dark, and expressionless, waited at the end of the hall. "That was less than satisfactory," he commented as he strolled by. "No dinner for her tonight."

"And tomorrow?"

He shrugged. "Use your judgement. It's her job to keep me happy, not the other way around." Climbing the stairs of his hideout, he entered his office. A hard copy of the investigative report he'd requested on Hale's latest conquest lay waiting on his desk, as anticipated. Flicking on his brass reading lamp, he sat down in his leather office chair to peruse it. The file contained numerous copies of photographs taken in Europe, mostly posed fashion shots. Brook had apparently been based in England for years, running a chain of boutiques.

No family. Oh, good. When she disappeared, there would be no whining relatives to complain except Hale and he might even be sick of her by then. He hoped not. Snatching her would be more fun if he pined over her absence. Mulling over the memory of their kiss at the event the other night, he felt certainty turn into doubt about Hale getting bored of her. It took a lot of incentive to make a stick in the mud like Hale make such an amorous demonstration in public.

He continued to read, shocked a few minutes later to discover she already resided in Gideon's home. That was a first, a more esteemed position than any woman in his life had held until now. It solidified the plans for his next attempt at overturning the other man's universe. He would snatch her away from him, take her in every way possible to punish both of them. Any potential schemes concerning the babbling idiot sister fled. Pampered little Tess was a mere child compared to this vital, enthralling woman who represented a worthy challenge. Ethan's perverse energy renewed, he closed the paltry file and headed back downstairs to quell his rapacious appetite once again.

Chapter Eleven

Brook wondered what was keeping Gideon, but she soon had her answer. Opening the kitchen door, he arrived while she and Tess were in the kitchen eating breakfast. Taking a seat across from Brook, he said, "Good morning, you two."

Tess raised an eyebrow. "What? All of a sudden, you're interested in eating breakfast? Since when?"

"It's a slow morning at the office so Neil and I decided to stay and have a bite with you two before we head in." Brook smothered a smile. She'd heard him cancelling an early meeting before she headed to her shower. That he would do such a thing pleased her in some obscure way. She doubted he did it very often.

"Where is he?" Tess asked.

"I'm here." Neil came in, smoothing his rebellious hair with one hand. "Morning."

Brook took note of the pleasure in Tess's face and stood. "How about cheese omelets? Everybody game?" At their assent, she went into the kitchen, only to find Gideon at her elbow.

"Allow me. Tess told me of your aversion toward meal preparation. Unlike you, I love to cook." Agreeing, she watched as he took the food out and started the necessary preparations with crisp efficiency. She pulled out plates, silverware, and glasses as he worked. At one point, Henry poked his head in to offer his help and his boss waved him away. With two pans in use, fifteen minutes later, everyone had a cheese and tomato omelet that smelled wonderful.

Brook provided the toast and poured juice for everyone. "You really do like to cook."

He nodded, following her to take a seat. "I do. I simply wish I could find more time for it. As it is, I usually just get a chance on weekends." The four of them ate and chatted, resulting in the guys leaving for the office almost an hour later than normal.

As soon as they heard the sound of the car pulling away, Tess plunked down in the opposite chair to face her and crossed her arms, her eyes twinkling. "Okay, fess up. What the heck is going on?"

"What are you talking about?" She tried for a look of innocence which wasn't an easy feat after what had happened between her and Gideon last night.

Her eyes narrowed. "My brother hasn't stopped for breakfast in over a decade. All of a sudden, he has time not only to cook and eat but to hang out. That never happens. Not until this moment, anyway."

"Am I being interrogated, Detective?" She waved at the light fixture above them. "Shouldn't that be glaring into my eyes?"

Tess thrummed her fingers on the table, staring at her with a speculative look. "Hmmm. I have a theory. Wait a minute." She leapt up and scurried away, letting the door bang against the wall as she exited the room. Brook heard her run up the stairs, each footstep thumping on the tread.

Where the hell was she going?

When Tess returned, she dropped into the chair, grinning from ear to ear. "You can crack jokes all you like, but it seems I'm quite a detective, after all. I've determined that I smell your cologne on his sheets. And there's a head dent on both of his pillows, not just one."

"Tess! Are you serious?" Her cheeks warmed with unaccustomed embarrassment.

She bubbled over with laughter, her delighted giggle filling the room. "I've never seen you blush before. It's hilarious. If I was really mean, I'd take a picture to show the guys."

Covering her face with her hands, Brook moaned. "You've finally managed to render me speechless."

"I knew it." Tess rubbed her hands together. "I haven't seen him look that happy in a long time. I want details."

"Absolutely not."

Laughter bubbled out. "Ewww. Not the physical stuff. He's my brother. No, I mean, how did it happen?"

Don't mention Ethan. "I can't explain it. We started playing our parts and our situation became more real than we expected." Brook shifted in her chair, unsure how to fully explain the change between them.

"It's so exciting." Her friend sighed. "My awesome brother is in love with my favorite secret agent."

Rolling her eyes, she said, "How about he's attracted to a federal agent, for a little dose of reality?"

"Close enough." Tess's teasing grin lit the room.

"Don't get carried away. Besides, I'm not sure how much longer Neil and I are going to stay at the Bureau."

"What? Really?"

She nodded. "The last year or so, Neil and I have been talking about starting a personal security firm. Spending your life on the road gets old after a while. We're kind of at a place when we both want something closer to a normal life."

"Will you settle here?" Without waiting for an answer, she continued gushing. "You'd love it and I'm here."

"I don't know yet. We haven't thought that far ahead. It's just we've been living this life for around fifteen years. It's been exciting, but I think the long hours and changing locations are getting old for both of us."

"The shrinks call it work/life balance. For selfish reasons, I hope you stay here. We could hang out all the time."

"That would be great, wouldn't it?" Brook shoved the enticing idea away for a moment. "Speaking of spending time together, what do you want to do today?"

Her plump lips turned downward in a parody of regret. "Charity luncheon downtown. Want to come? It promises to be deadly dull, but it's to support a really good music education program."

"Of course, I'm going to come. That's the deal, remember?"

"Oh, yeah. You're my guardian angel." She frowned. "Amelia Barnes is involved, but we'll have to hope she isn't present this time. Maybe we'll get lucky and she's busy somewhere else this morning."

Two hours later, they discovered that, of course, good fortune hadn't followed them. The meeting was held in the conference room of a downtown hotel. On entering the spacious room, Brook, staring at the overly ornate décor, didn't notice her nemesis approach them. A fake smile sat plastered on her face. Her teeth were blinding. *How much dental bleach does she use anyway?* Because they had an audience, there were air kisses all around before she moved on to a more receptive group.

The whole thing reminded Brook of a sorority meeting with the cool girls facing off with the outsiders. *I'm too old for this.*

They took small, cramped seats and were treated to a rather mediocre salad which they picked at while listening to some mind-numbing, long-winded speeches. *Sometimes, people just love the sound of their own voices.* She wondered how much time Tess spent honoring commitments like this. *It would drive me mad.* After a while, to guarantee she stayed awake, she excused herself to go to the restroom. Tess was surrounded by other women. No harm would come to her during the few minutes a rest stop would take.

When she emerged from the bathroom stall, Amelia stood at the counter, like a hungry cat waiting to pounce. Their gazes met in the mirror, the other woman's eyes shining with malicious intent. She ran a mascara wand over her lashes with a practiced hand. "It won't last, you know."

Oh, here we go. Brook took her time washing her hands. "I beg your pardon?"

"This little liaison you're enjoying with Gideon. You're just a shiny new toy that caught his eye. Before too long, he'll get bored and find his way back to me."

She took a leisurely minute to dry her hands, struggling to hide a grin. "I wouldn't count on that if I were you."

"He'll be happy to return to my bed. I've always satisfied him."

If this woman expected her choice of words to shock her, she was doomed to disappointment. Brook could speak fluent bitch. She dropped her soiled towelette into the waiting basket and turned to smile at her. "Actually, he prefers his own bed which is exactly where I'm living—in his bed, in his house. Believe me, there's no room left for you." She opened the door. "Enjoy your day." Exiting, she heard a curse, followed by a muffled shriek.

When she re-joined Tess, the endless meeting was coming to a close at last with people standing, chatting, in small groups. As they went to get their coats, Amanda sped by them, heels tapping a frantic tattoo, and whisked out the door. "What's with her?"

"I can't imagine," Brook replied, censoring herself because they could still be overheard.

"Brook—"

"Not here," she whispered. Once they made their way outside and entered the car, she told her what had happened, although not the specific words.

"Did you zing her good?"

"I believe you would be proud."

She didn't intend on mentioning it to Gideon, but, of course, Tess wouldn't have any part of that. Over dinner that night, she said, "Amelia cornered Brook in the bathroom at the luncheon today. I was mad I missed the show."

He put his fork down, turning in her direction with an air of concern. "What do you mean she cornered her?"

Tess answered before she could speak for herself. "It was a 'get your hands off my man' kind of thing."

Neil laughed and smothered it quickly when Brook glared at him. "Tess, seriously, let it go."

Clearly mortified, Gideon said, "I apologize for her inappropriate behavior. She doesn't take personal disappointments well, but these tantrums are getting ridiculous."

"That's an understatement," Tess replied. After a minute to process, they finished eating their meal and moved into the living room.

Gideon pulled Brook to one side as the other two searched through the entertainment center for a movie they wanted to watch. "Have you seen today's newspaper?"

"No, why?"

"There is an embarrassing article in the society column about us. I wanted to warn you."

"What does it say?"

"It's a photograph with a trashy headline." He winced. "Something along the lines of, 'Is this the new queen for the king of real estate?' "

"I didn't know you were royalty," she kidded, trying to get him to relax.

"The society column is often inappropriate." His face flushed and she found it endearing.

"You're embarrassed," she said, laughing. "Just ignore it. It suits our purposes. That's likely the reason for Amelia's outburst earlier."

"It's no excuse for such appalling behavior."

"Of course, it isn't, but I'm more than capable of dealing with a jealous woman."

"I've no doubt about that." He smiled. "I suppose you're right. You're a good influence on me. I need to learn to ignore such trivial things." They settled in and watched North by Northwest, apparently one of Tess's favorites. When it ended around eleven, Brook looked over to find that her friend had fallen asleep slumped against Neil's arm.

He tried to rouse her. "Good luck with that," Gideon joked. "She sleeps like the dead. I'll take her." He started across the room.

"I'll carry her." Neil's eyes darted to him. "With your permission, of course."

"Certainly."

He lifted her as you would a sleeping child, cradling her petite body against his chest. She mumbled and put her arms around his neck. She and Gideon followed Neil upstairs, watching as he laid her on the bed. Brook moved forward and covered her with the blanket on the end of her bed, tucking it around her. "She's in comfy clothes. She'll be fine," she whispered to the other two. They shut the door behind them and bade each other goodnight.

When she turned to go to her room, Gideon said, "Wait a moment," and disappeared into his room. When he returned, he had a newspaper in hand, open to the offending article. It showed a photograph of the two of them in the evening wear from the other night, smiling at each other, the ridiculous headline blaring above.

If she didn't know better, she'd swear they were a real couple. This wasn't the time to think about the ramifications of that. "It's a good picture of both of us, at least."

"This kind of inane coverage really doesn't bother you?"

She shook her head. "I think it's silly people care about such nonsense, but what can you do? Have a laugh and move on. Anything else is a waste of time."

"That makes sense. As I said, I always find that kind of article so intrusive." He paused. "I have an early meeting, so I'd better turn in, but can I ask you a question?"

"Of course."

"Does Neil like my sister? As more than a friend or a responsibility, I mean."

She sighed. "I promise you, he won't do anything about it. But, yes, I think so. Before we arrived, he called her pretty and they seem to get along well."

"Why wouldn't he ask her out? Is it our rather odd circumstances that are holding him back?"

Turning to face him, she said, "To be honest with you, he would consider Tess totally out of his league. He doesn't have a lot of confidence about relationships, either. Women always friend-zone him because, despite his appearance, he's quiet and sweet."

"You know she would never consider social standing a deterrent. It simply wouldn't occur to her."

"Maybe not, but I would bet he's more concerned about you than he is Tess. He's very proud, you know. He would never want to be seen as an opportunist."

He nodded. "I understand. I'll have to give that some thought. Maybe I can do something to help him get more comfortable with the idea."

His concern was another positive quality. They were certainly stacking up in his favor.

"That would be great."

"Did she ever tell you she was engaged?"

It surprised her that Tess had kept that tidbit to herself. "No, I had no idea."

"Not only did he cheat on her, but he had apparently been bragging about how she was his 'windfall' to everyone who would listen. Idiot. When she found out afterwards, she called herself a naïve fool and broke it off."

She felt a stab of pity. "I didn't know anything about that. How long ago was this?"

"Two years. She hasn't dated anyone since. Until Neil, she hasn't shown any interest in being with anyone."

"I don't blame her. Dating's the pits." Leaning up to kiss his cheek, she said, "Go to bed or you'll never make that meeting."

"Goodnight." He closed the door and she headed to bed.

Chapter Twelve

Gideon's tedious early meeting dragged on past its natural endpoint, but the rest of his morning flew by. At lunch hour, he was working out in the gym. "I wonder if you would do me a favor," he asked Neil, who had finished with the weights.

"Sure."

"Can you teach me how to shoot a pistol?"

Grabbing a towel, he wiped the trailing sweat off his face. "Of course. You remember Lieutenant Parker?"

"Yes."

"He'll let us on the police range. Kind of an inter-agency perk."

"And having me there won't be a problem?"

He laughed. "You pretty much have the keys to the city around here. Believe me, it won't be a problem. I'm assuming you want to learn for personal security, not sport?"

"That's right. I'd just as soon Tess didn't know, though. These days, I'd feel safer if I had a fallback plan."

Sobering, he agreed. "I think all this intrigue bothers her more than she says. She tries to stay so upbeat to keep everyone's spirits high."

Neil's insight impressed him. "That's the best summation of my sister than I've heard in years." Slowing, he turned off the treadmill. "Can we go to the shooting range after work?"

"Today?"

He nodded. "If you can set it up. I don't want to delay. I know it takes practice and I need to get started as soon as possible."

"Sure. I'll make a call while you're in your next meeting."

Later, after work, they stood together at the indoor range. Rubber mats covered every cement surface, the starkness making it clear that this was serious business. Neil explained the combination was to prevent ricochets. Each of the twenty spaces had a simple table at waist height on which to rest their equipment. Both men had changed back into their slightly sweaty gym clothes to be more comfortable. The only other shooters were at the opposite end of the line, so they could practice in relative privacy.

Neil had loaded a bag with their supplies, most of it borrowed from the local police force. He set it on the wooden surface in front of them, pulling out a pistol and laying it on the small mat he'd laid down. Explaining the need for eye and ear protection, he handed a set of each to him. "Don't worry about loading the gun for now. I'm going to show you how to stand and the proper grip to use first." He stood erect with his upper body slightly inclined forward and held his arms straight in a vee formation in front of him. "Like this." Picking up the gun, he turned to show how to wrap fingers around the grip. "Hold it snug. Any looseness will pull you off target." Relaxing, he asked, "Any questions so far?"

"No, that's clear."

"Okay. Now, we'll put on the eye and ear protection. I'm going to load up and shoot six rounds. I want you to step back a bit and watch how I squeeze the trigger." They paused to put on plastic safety glasses and heavy earmuffs.

Gideon watched, impressed, as the other man fired the six shots in an even cadence. Even from the seven-yard distance, he could see they were all in the center ring. "Impressive."

Neil grinned. "I've had a lot of practice." He handed him the gun and a fresh magazine of ammunition. "Now, you try. Remember, take your time. At this point, accuracy is way more important than speed." He stepped back. "For safety's sake, always assume the gun is loaded. When you're not shooting, keep it aimed down range with your finger off the trigger. And, when you shoot, use an even squeeze. Don't jerk it. It will pull you off target."

Gideon took his place, all of the rules running through his mind. He mimicked his friend's actions, sliding the clip into the gun and keeping the muzzle pointed down range. He lifted his arms and finessed his grip while letting the safety off with his thumb.

"Now, keep the gun level, so you can see the target between the two guides on the end of the gun. Your other option is to get a scope, but for now we'll work with iron sights."

He kept adjusting until he was comfortable, then nodded.

"You can shoot when you're ready."

Here we go. He squeezed the trigger and the gun fired, jumping a bit in his hand. Tightening his grip, he concentrated on the bullseye and the second shot was more accurate. He continued until the gun's slide locked back. Realizing with surprise he'd emptied the entire magazine, he lowered his arms. Neil gestured for him to lay the gun down on the mat which he did. Pushing a button beside him, they both waited as the target returned for them to inspect it. He could easily tell which bullet holes belonged to which man. Neil's were dead center, grouped with the borders touching, having almost torn the center away.

"This isn't bad," he said, looking at the other six bullet holes. "Half of yours are in the eight ring and half in the seven. That's a pretty good start." He tore the target off and replaced it with a fresh one. "We're looking for a tight grouping of shots, but that will take hours of practice. Consistency is important."

They took turns shooting for another hour with Neil suggesting slight changes in his position from time to time. In the end, Gideon was surprised his arms were so tired. He would have to add more weights to his workout. Glad to have his chauffeur drive, they relaxed on the way home. As they pulled up to the house, he said, "Let's try and sneak past the ladies so they won't guess where we've been by the cordite smell."

Neil nodded. "Back stairs?"

"Yes." They crept in like thieves in the night, but both men safely made it upstairs to their rooms. When they ventured back down after showering and changing, Tess jumped up from the couch. "We didn't even hear you guys come in. The sounds of the showers running surprised us."

"Sorry we kept you waiting for dinner. Is it ready?"

His question to distract them worked. Brook stood and waved everyone ahead of her. "Yes. It's keeping warm in the oven." Gesturing for them to sit down at the table, she moved a large, ceramic casserole dish to the table to join the crusty bread and salad that already waited. "Henry went out for the evening."

"To visit his girlfriend," Tess chimed in. Abe wandered in after they sat and she shooed him away.

"Where'd you guys go after work?"

"We had a drink with a client." That was the cover story they'd agreed to use. Gideon changed the subject to discourage any further questions.

They spent the evening watching television. After a while, Brook excused herself and went upstairs. She was taking a shower when she heard the bathroom door click open. Turning in that direction, she wiped the water from her face as footsteps sounded on the ceramic tile. Although her first instinct was to calculate how close she was to her gun, she recognized Gideon's shape. "In the mood for company?" he asked.

She could barely see him through the textured glass. Opening the door and crooking a finger in his direction, she said, "You'd better lose the robe. Although I should warn you, sneaking in to surprise me might have gotten you shot." She watched as he hung it on the back of the door and stepped in to join her.

"I'm sorry. That thought didn't even cross my mind. I'll be more cautious next time." The hungry kiss he gave her warmed her more than the shower had. Strong hands touched her everywhere and she returned the favor, still surprised his conservative suits hid this muscular body that so attracted her. When she would have continued, he turned off the water and wrapped her in a fluffy bath sheet, following suit. He reached over, tousling her hair with a spare towel. "My bed is bigger," he murmured, kissing her neck.

"But mine's closer." She pushed him backwards a

few steps, out the door, until they toppled onto the mattress together with her on top. All kidding ceased. Shoving the towels to the side, she began to tease him, nibbling his neck and venturing lower. "I missed you today."

He gasped, moving in to the contact. "I'll have to stay away more often."

"No. Don't." Changing position, she moved to straddle him, enveloping him. She set the rhythm, arching back, taking every bit of pleasure she could manage. The raging level of desire she felt shocked her. They moved together, sharing a language as old as time. He intuited her every need and she loved that he was so unrestrained in bed. No one would ever guess what passion lay hidden beneath the reserved personality he showed the outside world. She'd never experienced anything like this level of pleasure. It was her last dawning truth before their climax. Collapsed down next to him, she pulled his arms around her to rest.

He curled an arm around her shoulders as they lay, breathless, for long moments. "Promise me something."

A clutch of unfamiliar nerves took hold. "What?"

Turning to gaze into her eyes, he said, "No matter what happens in the future, for now at least, there won't be anyone else for either one of us."

Relief flooded her. She hadn't been sure what he was going to ask of her. "That's a simple decision. I'm very monogamous by nature. I agree."

"Good. Me, too." He smiled. "Now, let's go to my bed." Scooping her up with ease, he carried her across the hall to his room.

When she woke in the morning, he was gone. A small white card sat on the nightstand closest to her. It read, "Be careful. See you tonight." Such a sweet, simple gesture made her smile. The house was quiet as she crossed the hall to shower and dress. After that, she went downstairs to join Tess. She found her friend staring into the refrigerator. "What are you doing?"

"Trying to decide what to have for breakfast."

"Why don't I make us some eggs and toast?"

She rolled her eyes. "No offense, but boring," dragging the last word out for emphasis. Giving a happy little shriek of enthusiasm, she grabbed a tube from the rack door on the door. "Instant cinnamon rolls. Now, we're talking." Wearing pajamas with little dogs in party hats all over, she made quite a picture. She danced over to grab a baking sheet and some spray oil. Prying the unbaked treats out of their container, she paused to spray the oil on, turning one simple act into a theatrical performance. She placed them on the pan. "Ta Da," she announced before sliding them into the oven.

Her friend's simple enjoyment made Brook smile. "You know if I keep eating with you, I'm going to blimp out."

"Nah. You've got a lot of height to spread it over. You'll be fine."

"I'll take your word for it. If those beautiful dresses don't fit anymore, you can be the one to explain it to Gideon." As they waited for the buns to cook, Brook said, "You never told me you were engaged."

As if her comment had taken the gasoline from her engine, Tess spun slowly to face her, her expression sobering. "Yeah, no one likes to admit they were an idiot. Not even me."

"You're not an idiot to try and find love. It's what most of us want, isn't it?"

She shrugged. "Maybe you're stupid if you couldn't see what everyone else could tell at first glance. For some reason, you tend to think of a woman when you think gold-digger, not a man. I thought Gid was going to strangle him when he found out he'd been shooting his mouth off."

"I don't blame him. He knows you deserve so much more. Besides, if we kicked people off the earth for making a mistake about the opposite sex, there wouldn't be many of us left." She went over and hugged her. "If it makes you feel any better, Neil and I are pretty much dating rejects at this point. Neither one of us have had a steady relationship in years."

"I like Neil." A smile spread across her face and her eyes sparkled. 'He's sweet and thoughtful. And he has this sneaky sense of humor I adore."

"He likes you, too."

"Really?" She looked so hopeful, it warmed Brook's heart.

"Yes, really. He talks more to you than anyone else. You put him at ease and you always appreciate his gestures." The comment seemed to please her and she perked up, the jerk ex-fiancé once again in the rearview mirror where he belonged.

After breakfast with Tess, she reminded herself to try and be tactful, then checked in with her boss. "Are you making any progress with this case?" he asked, sarcasm coloring the words. "We can't continue to bleed money on this operation forever."

Brook could hear him tapping his pen against his desk, an annoying habit that made her want to shove the object up his nose or another, more sensitive, part of his anatomy. "We have an engagement this evening and

Ethan will be there. I'm going to turn up the heat and see what happens."

"You'd better do something. I can't have you living the high life at my expense."

Her blood pressure rose in response to his arrogant words and her free hand shook as she answered. "Most of the expense is at Gideon's hand, not yours or the Bureau's. If we rush it, he's going to catch on and we'll lose the upper hand." Grumbling a typical condescending response, he hung up. She gritted her teeth, turned off the phone, and located more pleasant company.

After she and Tess had lounged around for most of the day, chatting and playing board games, she asked her to help pick an outfit for the night. They eventually settled on a fitted black one-piece pantsuit, covered in sequins, a high, fitted neck in front and a plunging back, the material skating above her buttocks. "We'll put your hair up for this, but leave a few curling tendrils around your face."

"If you say so."

"I do." She circled around her, fussing with her hair, then finally finished. "There ya go. Sex on a stick." In the end, they had to hurry a bit on the drive over, because Gideon had been delayed at work. Luckily, the local theater where the event was being held wasn't too far away.

The evening performance was a charity night to support a group of young local musicians. It was the most fun she'd had out on the town with him. The leader of the band was the best trumpet player she'd heard in a long time. At intermission, she excused herself to visit the ladies' room while Gideon stayed in the lobby, catching up with some friends. As she returned to him, she came across Ethan lounging in the narrow hall, like a snake waiting to pounce. It wasn't hard to anticipate his intentions and she steeled herself not to overreact. She planned to nod her greeting and continue on her way, but he stretched an arm across to block her exit. "Not going to stop and say hello?"

"Good evening, Mr. Ames."

He tsk tsked, looking at her up and down in a degrading manner. "My, aren't we formal tonight. Surely, we're friends by now."

She cocked her head, envisioning how she could send him flying with one move. Keep in character, she admonished herself. "If I don't return, Gideon will wonder where I am. I don't like to keep him waiting."

"And does Gideon monopolize every precious moment of your time?"

Used to dealing with predators, she smiled, determined to bait him. "I am happy to have him do so." If he wasn't such a misogynist, he would hear the warning tone of her words.

Leaning forward, he grasped her upper arm and squeezed hard enough to leave a bruise. "You're wasting your time with him. I'm twice the man he'll ever be."

"Are you?" She lifted her chin, staring at him. "Forgive my skepticism. From my perspective, you're not even a distant second place."

His fingers clenched tighter, causing pain to snake up to her shoulder. As she debated what she could do that wouldn't give her role away, she heard Gideon's voice behind her, cutting through the dimness. "Get your hands off her." When Ethan did, he shoved him against the wall, causing a dull thud. The two men glared at each other, the arcing energy between them heated enough to cast sparks.

Moving to his side, she cautioned, "Darling, he's not worth it. Don't waste your energy." She tugged his arm. "I'm fine. Come on. Your friends are waiting for us." It was a tenuous moment, their panting breaths the only sound, then Gideon stepped away, taking her hand. She smothered a relieved sigh.

"You'll never hang on to her." Ethan chuckled as they walked away. He raised his voice to ensure his venomous taunt traveled down the hall behind them. "Women like her are meant to be underneath men like me." The ugly words echoed as they rejoined their group. They tried to enjoy the second half of the production, but the evening had been ruined by the confrontation. Gideon couldn't relax and suggested they slip out to head home. After valets delivered the car and they slid inside, the silence was deafening. She couldn't decide whether she should speak up or whether that would make things worse.

"He's a filthy pig." His words sounded both stilted and terse. She knew the fact that Ethan had put his hands on her had angered Gideon, could even feel his muscles tensing beside her. Only his admirable discipline had kept him from slugging the man. She considered that as the car pulled into traffic with a slight lurch that underscored his frustration.

"Yes, he is." How could she possibly disagree when even that was an understatement? "But he's trying to provoke you. Don't allow him to needle you into a regrettable response. You have an excellent reputation and he'd love nothing better than to ruin it."

"You could have had him writhing on the floor in an

instant. Why didn't you?" He turned the corner a little too fast. The tires squealed in belated protest.

"I couldn't indulge myself, although his behavior tempted me to do just that. But it would have blown my cover."

"How far would you have let him go?" The tense words sounded as if they'd been torn from him.

She felt a surge of empathy, knowing that their attraction made this even harder for him. "Not much farther."

He remained quiet until they entered his neighborhood, then he jerked the car to the curb and shoved the gear shift into park. Yanking her toward him, he kissed her, hard, his anger morphing into passion. She kissed him back, softening it in an effort to soothe him. After a moment, he pulled away and swore. "I'm sorry. This incessant needling is so much more than I bargained for. I'm not dealing with the constant pressure as well as I'd hoped."

"Don't be so hard on yourself. You're doing fine under trying circumstances."

"Am I? It doesn't seem like it." He put the car back in gear and proceeded home at a slower pace. They left the car in the garage and entered the house without another word. She couldn't think of a way to comfort him at first. Back in her own room, she changed out of her clothes and slipped into a nightgown. His bedroom door stayed closed, but she rapped on it anyway, then opened it.

"I'm not very fit company tonight." He stared at her from his position on the bed, his tension showing in his rigid jaw.

He needed her and, despite the brevity of their

relationship, she knew it. "Would you rather I went to my own room?"

"No, never that. Your company is always desired, although I'm not sure I deserve it tonight."

That's all she needed to hear. Shutting the door behind her, she joined him in bed as he lay back. He moved onto his side and met her gaze. "How do you always stay so serene when I'm a wreck?"

She curled into the crook of his arm. "You forget that I've done this job for years. Your first glimpse of our life was a terrifying one. I'd worry about your intelligence if you found it commonplace."

"How do you deal with the stress?"

She tried to phrase her response in a way that would resonate with him. "I always focus on the end result. That's catching the bad guy and making him pay the price. It's a pretty great feeling when your hard work pays off and justice prevails."

"And when it doesn't?"

She shrugged. "Then, it can be really tense for a while. But nothing in life is perfect."

"You are. You're perfect."

He said it with such a solemn air, she laughed. "Not even close. I can't cook or sew and I don't really care, so I'd fail any domestic test you could offer. And I get bored easily, which is why this job always worked well for me."

"You said worked in the past tense."

"Did I?" She smiled. "Slip of the tongue." She didn't want to talk about the uncertainties of the future tonight. Moving over to lie against him, she gave him a kiss and ran one hand down his chest.

"Are you trying to distract me?"

"Absolutely. Is it working?"

"I don't know." He moved his hands to her butt, stroking. "You might have to try a little harder."

"Be glad to." She rubbed her body against his like a cat, hearing him suck in a breath. "Oh, you haven't seen anything yet. And, by the way, let me be the first to wish you Happy Birthday."

Chapter Thirteen

The next morning, she barely managed to scrabble back to her room before she heard Tess bounce into Gideon's suite, shouting Happy Birthday. She heard his laughing response as she stepped into the shower. When she came back out of the bathroom, her towel wrapped around her, Tess waited on the edge of her bed. "Hmmm. Funny how your bed's always made first thing in the morning." She snickered. "Who do you guys think you're fooling?"

"Honestly, Tess. Don't embarrass him." She searched out fresh clothes from the closet.

"It's my duty as his sister." She pointed to her watch. "Tick tock. Henry's making birthday breakfast as we speak."

"I'll be down in five minutes."

She hurried to the door. "I'll hold you to it."

"Is Neil up yet?"

"We've been up for ages," she said before disappearing out the door. The use of the word "we" didn't escape her notice. *Interesting.*

They all congregated in the kitchen, drawn by the amazing aroma of freshly baked goods. Fragrant rolls and croissants sat next to a huge plate of assorted fruit. Henry was busy preparing quiche and bacon for everyone. The tantalizing mix of aromas made her stomach gurgle in anticipation. Before they ate, they sang Happy Birthday to Gideon, dreadfully off-tune and all the more memorable for it. Afterwards, Tess shouted, "Speech, speech."

Smiling, Gideon said, "There's nowhere else I'd rather be on my birthday than here and no other four people that I'd rather be with. Now, let's eat before the food gets cold." They greeted his words with a cheer and dug in. After everyone was stuffed to the gills, he opened his gifts. Besides the robe and chocolates, Henry had given him a leather picture frame with a picture of the four of them he had taken last week. The festivities were interrupted by the chiming of the front doorbell. Henry excused himself to answer it. After a moment, he called Brook out into the hall. She hurried out to find him setting a huge flower arrangement on the table, a small, white card in his hand. Who would send Gideon flowers, she wondered, then was startled by Henry's words. "They're for you," he said, handing her the card. "I wasn't sure where you'd like me to put them."

Confused about who would have sent them, she looked at the card. It read: You belong beneath me. It was signed with an oversize E. Nausea threatened, making her gulp. "Throw them out." She struggled with the order, her voice trembling. "The vase, too. And don't let Gideon see them."

"That's an expensive arrangement. Are you certain?"

"Yes, Henry. Please, as fast as you can. These are a taunt from a man we both despise. It will only upset Gideon and ruin his special day." She hurried back into the kitchen before anyone questioned her absence.

"What did Henry want?" Gideon asked.

She forced a smile. "Now, don't spoil his birthday

plans for you. He'll be most upset." The answer satisfied him, but she hated fibbing, even if it was to protect him. There didn't seem to be any point in telling him about the crass gesture and spoiling the day.

They spent the afternoon playing games in the garden; first badminton and then touch football. She tried to remember the last time she and Neil had time for a fun afternoon of games and couldn't. Had they ever? It gave her some insight to what it might be like to live a more normal life. Later in the day, she found a quiet moment to tell Neil about the flowers. Texting the same information to her boss brought a reply that said, "It's about time. What now?"

A great question. The more she considered it, the more she realized that she wanted this case over with as soon as possible. The other team members felt the same way. It had dragged on far longer than it should have. The sheer worry of their unusual predicament tormented Gideon. And being with him made her feel like the time had come to get on with her life. The ongoing years couldn't all be about work. *Not anymore.*

She shoved her concerns about their complicated situation away for the rest of the day so she could enjoy the positively sinful birthday dinner Henry had prepared. He'd paired a mouth-watering steak that melted in your mouth with grilled potatoes and asparagus. An amazing chocolate mousse cake followed. After the lengthy meal, Gideon pushed himself away from the table, groaning. "Thank you, Henry. You've outdone yourself, as always."

"You're welcome." He gave a mock bow. The others offered to do the dishes so he could have the evening off.

The next day they spent the laziest Sunday she could ever remember and it was heavenly. They ate breakfast, then watched old movies, all four nestled up on two couches. Tess curled up against Neil who looked unsure about whether that was okay before he finally relaxed. At one point, Brook realized her friend hadn't really fallen asleep when she winked at her, then snuggled in even more. Her friend was making a play—it was sweet. Neil needed some encouragement.

After Gideon arrived home from work the next day, Brook cornered him in his bedroom for a talk. "I think I know how to edge this case toward a conclusion, but I need your help. It's an unorthodox solution, but I think it might work."

He sat down, concern darkening his eyes. "Okay. I have to admit I'm afraid to ask what you're up to now."

She blew out a breath, knowing he wouldn't like it. "I think we should shop for engagement rings at your favorite jewelry store. We have a source who will leak it to the press. You don't have to buy anything, just make it clear to everyone we're in the market."

"Brook—"

She shrugged. "I know. It's awkward as hell and it means more publicity which I know you hate, but this situation can't go on forever. It's wreaking havoc in all of our lives. I want that bastard off the streets so we can wrap up this case at last."

"It's too risky. It's like painting a big, red target on your back, then taunting a pawing bull."

She moved over to kiss his cheek. "High risk, high rewards. As a businessman, you know that kind of planning can yield a very satisfactory result. We'll take every precaution to ensure everyone's safety."

"When would we do this?"

Noting the look of resignation on his face, Brook edged closer. She touched his arm, feeling his muscles tense under her fingers. "Day after tomorrow. That will give us the time to put all the pieces in place."

"I don't really have any say in this, do I? I simply despise the level of risk you're taking on."

She shook her head, feeling guilty that, in the short term, she'd be adding to his stress level. "Try to trust our process. I know all the deception is hard to bear, but I need your help to end this. Concentrate on how happy we'll all be when it's over and he's behind bars."

"And what about us?" He lifted her chin with one finger and stared into her eyes. "How do we move forward? Or do we?"

"I hope we do. Ultimately, I guess that's up to you."

He kissed her, his lips persuasive. "I haven't ever felt this kind of connection with anyone. I want to find a way to make a relationship work."

"Well, then, we will. Remember that's the ultimate goal. The rest of this is just business."

He let it go, but she knew their path took its toll on him. Picking up the phone, she began putting the pieces in place.

Two days later, they strolled hand in hand into the most expensive jewelry store in town. The owners had agreed to keep it open an extra hour, just for them. A call earlier in the day had guaranteed it. The exhilarated manager fell all over himself, serving them personally. They scanned a collection he'd hand-picked as the best of the best. She could only guess at the expense involved. Scanning the trays, she was amazed at the unusual settings. When she asked the price of the first ring she tried on, Gideon laughed. "Darling, don't concern yourself. The only thing that matters is that you choose something you love." Despite his earlier concerns, he seemed to derive pleasure from watching her try on an assortment of rings, nodding at some and shaking his head at others.

She made a big production of hemming and hawing over the various choices, surprised she enjoyed the process. *A first time for everything.* Could she have felt comfortable pretending with anyone, but him? *Not likely.* When the skulking photographer shot a picture of them through the front window, she pretended not to notice. She had to drool over one choice—a square cut diamond with a unique engraved band. Gideon spoke to the manager in undertones and she was pleased he played his part to the hilt. She pointed out the ones she liked and disliked. They left it at that with Gideon telling the manager he would be back.

Sure enough, the next morning, the headline in the society column was, *Is Gideon Hale off the marriage market?* They had to warn Tess about what they were doing and, true to form, she insisted on acting as if the charade were true.

****

Stalking around his spacious penthouse in the city, Ethan re-read the headline in the morning newspaper in disbelief and tossed it aside. "Are you serious?" he muttered to himself, cursing under his breath. Hale had never been engaged. The bevy of local socialites who'd thrown their daughters in his path were appalled at the idea of a man with so much money running free. That solitary fact made him the subject of a constant scheme to bag him and drag him to the altar. He'd eluded them thus far, much to their ongoing chagrin. This new development about a search for a ring indicated how serious he was about Brook. Had Ethan sending her the bouquet of flowers pushed him into this engagement? Was the pathetic bastard that scared of losing her to another man?

The shopping expedition accomplished one thing, though. That one move clarified his own plans. It was time to snatch his tempting paramour now, before she became even more embedded in Gideon's life. The couple would be distracted by their upcoming nuptials and the fuss it would cause with the press. It would make it much easier for him to make his final move.

But how? His plan would have to be foolproof down to the last letter, unlike the failed escapade with Gideon. He envisioned how delicious it could be to spoil her for any decent man. The mere possibility of devouring her raised his unholy appetite to ravenous heights.

With sadistic devotion to his evil intent, he began to formulate an ultimate plan.

Chapter Fourteen

Hard at work at his desk the following day, Gideon paused when Enid buzzed him. "Sorry to interrupt, sir. Ethan Ames is on the line and wishes to speak to you."

That's the last thing I need today. "Tell him I'm in a meeting and can't be disturbed, please."

"Yes, sir." After she ended the conversation, he wondered for a moment what that man could possibly want. Shaking his head, he returned to work.

When Enid came in later to collect some signatures, he asked, "Did Ames say what he wanted?"

She frowned. "It's a little peculiar, sir. He said, 'Ask him if Brook liked the flowers I sent her.' I'm afraid I wasn't clear about the reference, but he hung up when I asked for clarification."

He glanced over at Neil who sat in one corner of the office. His transparent expression showed uncomfortable guilt. "Thank you, Enid." Handing her back the stack of signed papers, he waited until she closed the door behind her. "What's this about him sending her flowers?"

The other man sighed, meeting his gaze. "The bastard sent a big bouquet with a sleazy note to her on your birthday. She had Henry throw it all out before you could see it. She didn't want it to ruin your day and knew you'd be upset."

"Damn straight. Who the hell does that bastard think

he is?"

"He's not a good loser and knows he'd never have a chance with her. He's trying to shake things up. Don't let him."

He understood Brook's intentions, but he didn't like being blindsided. "I won't. I wished she'd told me, though. I don't like being left in the dark." It helped him make up his mind on another matter he'd been mulling over. He asked Neil to excuse him while he made a call. When he returned, Gideon mentioned they would have one quick stop to make on the way home.

****

As Gideon lay in bed next to Brook that night, he said, "I heard about the flowers that monster sent you on my birthday. He called the office to ensure that I found out about it."

She leaned over and stroked his arm to make amends. "I'm sorry I didn't tell you. I didn't want it to ruin your birthday celebration. There's nothing you could have done about it, anyway."

"I called Parker to discuss Ethan's obsession with you. We agreed that he seems to be upping his game when it comes to tormenting us. He reiterated what you'd said to me—that there are pros and cons to that scenario."

"Did he have any suggestions about what to do about it?"

"Not really. He said that he'd remind everyone to keep up their guard, that things might be coming to a head. And he encouraged me to let you and Neil handle the details."

"I know that's difficult for you. You prefer to be in control of every situation and I don't blame you."

He frowned. "That makes me sound like a cave man, but, I'm afraid it's true. I like to feel in control of my life."

She laughed and the sound of it lightened his mood. "I prefer to think of trying to take care of people as chivalrous. You appear to respect both me and my career, so you're not a cave man. I have no complaints."

"Glad to hear it. I'll attempt to keep it that way and give you the reins for a while." When she reached for him, he realized that letting her distract him in a time-honored way would be in both of their best interests.

****

After a long day at work the next day, Gideon showered, changed, and called Brook into his bedroom. After closing the door for privacy, he handed Brook a small, black velvet box. She recognized the logo from the jewelry store on its top.

Frowning, she asked, "What is this?"

"Open it."

Her hand trembling, she did as he asked. Inside was the sparkling, square cut diamond she'd admired in the store. She looked at him, a confused expression on her face. "I told you that you didn't have to actually buy anything. This is crazy expensive. I know it is."

"I want you to wear it anyway. It will help both of us focus on a future after this fiasco is over and done." He touched her cheek, letting his fingers trail down her neck. "I need that right now. I need to believe that we'll all get through this unscathed." She watched, thunderstruck, as he slipped it on her left hand. It fit perfectly. "I borrowed one of your other rings and had it sized."

"That was clever. I'm impressed at how quickly you

managed to get this done."

He shrugged. "I'm not nearly as exciting as you, but I have my moments." Having her in his life made him feel alive in a way he hadn't for years. Sometimes, he allowed work and other responsibilities to force out more pleasurable experiences. It was a fault he planned to work on starting now.

Leaning in, she kissed him. "It's stunning. Thank you."

When they returned downstairs, Tess noticed at once, racing forward to stare. "Jeez, that thing's a boulder!" She bubbled on and on about it to Henry who looked amused at her enthusiasm.

After a few minutes, Neil pulled her aside and bent down to whisper in her ear. "I thought buying a ring was just pretense."

"So did I."

"And…"

"He wants it to be a symbol of a better future for all of us after this case is over."

"Well," he said, glancing at Tess with a softening look in his eyes. "I guess I can understand that. When he stopped at the jewelry store yesterday, I wondered what he was up to."

While both men were busy at work the next day, Brook offered to show Tess some basic self-defense moves in the backyard. "You remember you said you wouldn't know what to do if you were attacked? Well, I can show you some helpful moves."

Looking skeptical, she said, "Some lame, short people stuff? The kind that makes midgets like me feel included, but doesn't really do anything to help?"

Brook tried to look indignant at her doubt and failed.

"It's true that petite people often have to use different tactics than someone my height, but you might be surprised." Leading the way outside onto the thick, green lawn, she turned to face her, taking a broad stance. "First of all, if you can run, always do that rather than fight. Don't try to be a hero. Always take the easiest solution."

"I'm no chicken." She puffed her chest out and Brook struggled to keep a straight face. The fact that she looked like a determined kid was something she'd keep to herself.

"It's not about being a chicken. It's simple common sense."

"I know. I'll bet even Gid would have run if he'd recognized the threat in time."

"I would hope so. Anyway, since you're small, you should be aware that a man might try to pick you up and carry you. What would you do then?"

"Kick 'em in the balls," she muttered, a manic delight in her expression accompanying the phrase.

"That's great in theory, but it doesn't usually work in practice. It can be hard to reliably reach...up there. Instead, use two fingers and aim for the eyes or the throat." She demonstrated while Tess watched. "Keep them straight—like a prong."

She looked less than impressed. "That seems like nothing more than those old vintage comedians who used to poke each other all the time."

"Not if you can dislodge an eyeball or fracture their larynx. You have to put some force behind it. Like it's a real punch."

She looked a little nauseated at the thought. "That's kinda gross."

Brook narrowed her eyes to make a point. "And if it

means the difference between you being abducted or staying safe?"

Hunching over, she tried for a threatening expression with bared teeth and ended up looking like a crazed bunny instead. "Then those eyeballs are coming out. One, two, plop, plop—they're outta here."

She tried not to laugh at her friend's version of an attack. "Okay, great. The idea is to do something they can't anticipate. Just because you look like a porcelain doll doesn't mean you can't assert yourself. Use the element of surprise."

"This stuff should be taught to every girl in high school." She jabbed her hand out, practicing.

"I agree."

She relaxed. "Have you ever had to use this stuff to defend yourself?"

"Yes. More than once. In my job, you always need to be aware of your surroundings. If the bad guys manage to get you into a car, your chances of survival go down by eighty percent."

Her face paled. "What do you do if, despite your best efforts, they get you into the car?"

"Go full throttle. Grab the wheel and crash into something or jump out, rolled in a ball, even if the car's moving. Attract the attention of another motorist." She patted her on the back. "The hard part for females is that women are raised to be kind and nurturing. Bad guys often take advantage of that instinct. If something terrible happens, you have to shove that part of you aside and get aggressive."

"You mean think more like a man?"

"Exactly. I couldn't have said it better myself."

They spent a couple of hours practicing evasive

maneuvers that could work for someone of her size, using simple momentum. After all that exercise, they were both sweaty and tired. They hit the showers, changed into comfortable clothes, and sat down in the kitchen with glasses of wine. Tess took a sip. "I think Neil is teaching Gid to shoot."

"Why do you say that?"

"Henry had Gid's clothes piled next to the washer and some of them had that weird smell gun ammunition makes." She narrowed her eyes. "You knew, didn't you? Why didn't anyone tell me?"

Brook sighed. "No one wanted to worry you. We are all trying to have every advantage going in our favor right now. As boring as it sounds, being prepared is always the most important component of success."

"That's why you wanted to teach me this stuff."

"Yes."

"Should I get a gun?"

"No, I think that's going overboard. It's harder than you think and it would just add to your stress. Trust me. Between all of our skills, we'll be fine." Tess stayed quiet for a while after that and only cheered up again after Neil showed up.

****

After the local realtor's meeting had broken up, Ethan waited until everyone left and approached a woman sitting on the other side of the restaurant, glaring. He'd recognized Hale's spurned girlfriend, Amelia Barnes, sitting there the entire time, drooling over Gideon. He, on the other hand, appeared to have ignored her and left through the back door to avoid her, his oaf of a security guard following. Ethan couldn't resist poking the bear, so to speak.

146

"Amelia, good to see you." He didn't wait for an invitation, simply slipping into the opposite seat. "What are you doing here today?"

She snapped her purse shut with a frown. "Why don't you find someone else to needle?"

"I guess you were just enjoying the view." He leaned closer. "He doesn't want you, sweetheart. Hasn't he made that crystal clear?"

"If I'd known he wanted a bimbo who lays around all day, I wouldn't have wanted him in the first place." Her usually pretty face didn't look so pretty now with a petulant pout marring her lips.

"Oh, I'm sure she does something worthwhile to earn her keep. I can hazard a guess as to what that is." He chuckled at the sight of her cheeks turning fiery red.

"She and his little twit of a sister lounge around the garden half the day. I've seen them sitting around, doing nothing."

He cocked his head. *Interesting.* "Are you parked at the end of their driveway with binoculars now? That may be a little over the top, even for you."

She stood up so quickly her chair almost tumbled over. With a few choice curses, she stomped away, leaving other patrons staring after her. Well, that had made his day. And, as he exited himself, the limited information she'd provided gave him an idea.

An hour later, he was in a rented car, passing the Hale property. Getting through the neighborhood gate had been a breeze. He just told the guard he was looking at a house that was for sale a few properties up. The policeman was gone from Hale's private gate, but he wasn't taking any chances at being recognized. He couldn't afford to drive by more than twice or a neighbor might notice. As he passed it, he found himself surprised. For heaven's sake, the house couldn't be more than seven or eight thousand feet. Why wouldn't he buy something more impressive than some rambling house? He could afford much more. *Idiot.*

Up at the higher end of the street, he found an angle that allowed him to see Hale's large back lawn. It trailed a longways to the rear fence and had large shade trees on the perimeter. After checking that out, he circled out to check the street which ran behind the property. A more concrete plan took shape. He began to whistle a jaunty tune, happy that his idea would work. This productive day just kept getting better and better.

****

After supper, Gideon excused himself to do some work he'd brought home from the office. Tess had a headache and went upstairs to pop a few painkillers, then take a nap. Restless, both Brook and Neil wandered out to the garden so their conversation wouldn't disturb the others. They collapsed into the comfy teak chairs with a sigh. Neil glanced around. "I really like this place, but it's not what you'd expected a loaded guy to own, is it?"

"What do you mean?"

"I mean it's homey. Like there's nice stuff everywhere, but it's not like a museum."

She nodded. "I know what you mean. That was my first thought after we moved in." Pausing, she took a breath of the clean, cool air and let it out. "I'm glad you're comfortable here. I worried that you might feel weird about it."

"Tess makes it easy. And Gideon too, of course."

She hid a smile. "You really like them, don't you?"

"Hard not to. They're not snobby at all, which is

surprising because they've always had money."

"And do you like Tess in particular?"

He was quiet for so long, she didn't think he would answer, then he did. "You know I'm crappy at that kinda stuff. And I don't want to make her uncomfortable."

"She told me she really likes you."

"Yeah?" Even in the dim light, she saw a smile form on his face. "Maybe when this is all over, I could ask her out. Do you think Gideon would mind?"

"Why would he? You're a great catch. If you're worried about it just talk to him. After her engagement, I think she gave up on finding someone, but she's really happy around you."

"The feeling's mutual."

"Good." They talked about work for a few minutes, but then Gideon and Tess showed up and invited them in to watch a show.

****

Ethan watched as his head man shut the door of the office behind him. The plans to take Hale's woman had been finalized and he felt ready to celebrate at last. They would never see him or his men coming. He would whisk her right out from under that insufferable man's nose. All the police and FBI agents would be left running in circles like clowns in a circus. The other women he'd taken were hors d'oeuvres compared to the scrumptious meal he would enjoy at the end of this brilliant case of misdirection. He would grab Brook, then steal everything from her, and there wasn't anything that pompous ass could do about it.

His success all came down to perfect timing, something on which he prided himself. He'd hired true mercenaries this time, not street thugs, so he had a small army of men to rely on, men whose consciences were bought and paid for by his overseas account. And he had a carefully thought-out fallback plan as well, in case a hasty retreat was necessary for him to escape. Best of all, he'd chosen the perfect property on which to imprison her, one that they'd never consider until it was too late to save her. The poetic justice of it made him smile. The huge, old, abandoned factory had more escape routes than a damn maze.

And, once she was in hand, he had a delightful celebration planned for the two of them, one that would offer forbidden experiences she would take to her grave.

Chapter Fifteen

Brook woke with an ominous feeling chilling her bones. Try as she might, she couldn't shake the sense of foreboding that slithered down her spine. When Gideon left for his morning meeting, she told him to be careful twice, causing him to look at her with concern. He'd asked if she was all right. She'd plastered on a smile, hoping he didn't notice the forced nature of it, and reassured him she felt fine. But that marked the first lie she'd ever told him.

She'd always had a sixth sense while working a case, one that had saved her and Neil more than once. So, she didn't ignore it. Whispering in Neil's ear for them to keep a close watch, she watched them leave for the office. She noted the look of concern on his face just before he said, "Stay sharp," and closed the door behind him.

She felt conflicted. In one way, she wanted to get this fiasco over with as soon as possible. On the other hand, she had to ensure that Tess and Gideon stayed safe at all costs. How could she manage that while waiting on tenterhooks for the ax to fall?

Through breakfast, she listened to Tess chatter, struggling not to let her heightened anxiety show. It was a rare, quiet day with nothing planned. The gathering clouds in an otherwise sunny day seemed like another omen. After they dressed in comfortable clothes, she suggested they go out to the yard for some fresh air. Maybe a look around would reassure her. But, instead of the sweet, fragranced air making her feel better, the hair on her arms rose in instinctive warning. Glancing around casually, she realized one of the fence panels looked as if it had shifted a little to the left. The only change she'd noted, but it was enough of a warning. She steeled herself and turned to face her friend, speaking up. "Do you mind getting us some snacks and a drink? I'm a little tired for some reason. I think I'm just going to sit and enjoy the sun." She took a seat at the far end of the lawn, facing away from the fence and closed her eyes. *Please just do as I ask.*

Tess hesitated and Brook felt a clutch of fear. *Oh, God, Tess. Move!* "Are you feeling okay?"

"Yes, I'm fine. I don't know why I'm so hungry this morning."

With that prompt, Tess finally headed back to the kitchen as Brook watched through slitted eyes. "You're used to Henry's fab cooking, that's why," she called over her shoulder. When Brook heard the glass door click closed behind her, she breathed a sigh of relief.

Okay, you bastards. Come and get me.

****

Ten minutes later, Tess came back out to the yard, balancing the laden tray of goodies on one arm. "Brook, can you shut the door for me?" Silence greeted her. *She must have fallen asleep.* She spun slowly around, scanning the lush garden. Still no response. She peeked under the big willow and called, "Brook?" Getting annoyed, she set the tray down on a table. After stomping down to the far end of the yard, she took a minute to scan the entire lawn area. A few birds twittered, but, otherwise, silence reigned. Had her friend gotten past her and returned to the house? The seat she'd been sitting on sat empty. In fact, it had toppled onto its side.

Beside it, she caught sight of something on the ground. Glittering prisms sparkled in the sunlight. Her stomach dropped as she reached down and pulled the item free of the blades of grass.

Brook's engagement ring. She gasped in a few sucking breaths, then screamed, the unbalanced shriek ringing in her ears.

Henry came running.

****

Having given the chauffeur the rest of the day off, Gideon was driving home with Neil when Henry called, his frantic words stilted. "Miss Brook is missing. I've summoned Lieutenant Parker."

"What happened?" Changing lanes with a jerk of the wheel, he hit the gas, squealing through a late yellow light.

"She disappeared from the back lawn. Tess was in the kitchen for just a few moments and returned to find her chair toppled over and her ring lying in the grass. I've checked everywhere, including the neighbors. She's nowhere in sight."

"We're fifteen minutes away. Stay locked inside the house and don't leave Tess's side." After filling Neil in, neither of them spoke as they careened around the other vehicles in their path. They finally arrived home twelve minutes later, leaving the car on the drive. Leaping out, they ran into the house.

Henry sat on the couch in the family room, cradling a hysterical Tess. Lieutenant Parker and another officer had been close by when called and had beaten them there. They stood talking into cellphones. He went to his knees beside his sister. "Did you see anything?"

Tess shook her head, swiping aside falling tears with one trembling hand. "I was only inside for a few minutes. I never heard a thing." She sucked in a breath and huffed it out again. "Brook was on the lawn, talking, then she was…gone. It's all my fault. I should have stayed with her."

Neil moved to stand beside her. "Of course, it's not your fault. You didn't do anything wrong."

"I left her alone."

"And, if you would have been there, they would have taken both of you." Henry moved closer and wrapped his arms around her.

Parker slid his cellphone in his pocket. "A van was seen parked on the next street over from here. It was white with no markings. If that was them, they had to haul her through the back fence." He hurried outside and crossed the lawn as Gideon and Neil followed. They perused the area Tess had indicated she found the ring. On the far outside of the lawn, they found a large fence panel had been cut free, then put back into place. Jagged cuts through the metal bore testament to what had happened. The tall, surrounding trees gave enough shelter that the threat of detection was minimal. On the neighbor's lawn, they found a spot where the grass was flattened as if something had been dragged across its surface. When they followed the resulting trail to the street, they found an earring close to the curb.

Gideon nodded, feeling nauseated. "It's hers. She must have left it behind for us to find." He tried to stifle his rising panic. Prayers that she could handle this safely ran a loop through his brain.

When they returned to the house, Officer Smith said, "They've set up a ten-block radius, but, so far, no sign of an unmarked white van." Gideon looped an arm around Tess's shoulders as she wept, gasping for breath. Neil sat on her other side, holding her hand.

"What do we do now?" He waited for any advice her partner or anyone else could offer.

****

Brook feigned unconsciousness in order to gain some time to figure out her options. Whatever they'd injected into her arm hadn't taken effect until they threw her in the back of the van. Luckily, she hadn't stayed unconscious for long. She peered through her lashes to get a useful perspective of the utilitarian room which now imprisoned her, careful not to move her head and alert the guards. About fifteen feet square, her temporary jail had no windows to help her guess the building's location. The unyielding cot they'd thrown her on was the only piece of furniture besides one wooden framed chair pushed against the shabby cement block wall. If she was left alone, even for a moment, she could smash the chair and use a jagged piece of it as a weapon. One large nail or screw could also do a lot of damage if necessary. Either that or the metal spring that currently dug into her back. She had tools she could use. Now, she needed an opportunity to use them.

Straining to listen, all she could hear was the low muttering of the two hulking men who stood guard by the door. Former military—she could tell by the tattoos on their arms. *Mercenaries*. He'd obviously learned to stay away from the band of street thugs who failed him last time.

Ames himself hadn't as yet made an appearance.

How much time did she have left to figure out an exit strategy? Did he intend to rape her, kill her, or both? At this point, despite appearances to the contrary, she realized she had a huge advantage. Confident that he was dealing with a pampered debutante, he wouldn't expect someone with her extensive training. Thinking in terms of a positive outcome was an important part of her education. Her mindset didn't pose a question of could she get out, but rather exactly how she would manage to escape this madman. Tiny shivers of doubt tried to sneak in, but, resolute, she shoved them away. In one way or another, the future of all four of them was at stake.

As if considering the difficult questions had conjured Ethan, the heavy door creaked open to admit him. The guards stood back to let him pass, watching him with some trepidation, their eyes downcast. He appeared as if he had dressed for a business dinner, every elegant hair lacquered in place. His appearance contrasted wildly with the starkness of the room.

She eased her eyes shut and tried to relax her limbs. Crossing the floor, he came and lowered himself to sit on the edge of the sagging mattress. "Now, darling, we all know you're awake." When she didn't respond, he slapped her across one cheek, the sound shocking against the relative silence. Feeling the harsh, heated imprint he left on her skin, she opened her eyes, but said nothing.

"There you are. You have such expressive eyes. I had hoped you'd be dressed in something more enticing, but I can remedy that. I require all my lovers to be beautifully attired."

Might as well deal with the painful reality right away. "You can rape me, but I'll never be your lover. The only man I'll ever truly desire is Gideon."

He smiled and his gleeful expression chilled her to the bone. She forced herself not to pull away when he splayed a hand on her chest. "We'll see about that, won't we? I'll be more than thrilled to prove you wrong." When she didn't respond, he smirked. "Nothing more to say? Don't worry, my love. Soon, your mouth will be far too occupied to speak." Squeezing her breast hard enough to cause pain, he stood and sauntered back through the door. He slammed it shut behind him. The sound reassured her that, whether his words revealed it or not, her defiant responses could still get to him.

She knew he wanted to hear her whimper in pain and refused to give him the satisfaction. It was what the other women had done, she guessed, and it had eventually led to their demise. She'd studied monsters like him and knew what made him tick. Her only chance of surviving him meant showing no sign of weakness or real emotion, no matter how severe the physical pain or emotional torment. She'd been badly injured before this episode. The trick was to survive it or die trying. Oh, Gideon, she thought with profound regret. *I'm so sorry I may not live through whatever's coming.*

****

Back at the house, Gideon and Neil watched all the bustling activity from a distance. Holstein was out of town and would be delayed getting here which seemed the only blessing in this mess. They both felt helpless as Parker checked through the long list of Ames's property holdings. The building where Gideon had been held had been checked and was vacant. The few pieces of real estate Ethan owned that had sizable acreage and were outside the city were being checked out as possible holding sites. With no real proof of who'd taken Brook, they'd need a warrant to take the investigation of those properties further. So far, they'd only been able to check out the properties from outside their perimeters. They were all hoping desperately for some piece of information that would help narrow the large number of choices down.

Neil stood and walked away from the others to stare out of the window. After a moment, Gideon joined him. "What are you thinking about?"

"Brook is the one who's great about getting into a suspect's head. I'm trying to think the way she does. She would ask where this particular suspect would be likely to take a victim and why."

"They're already checking out his properties, at least enough to know if they're vacant."

He rubbed his hands over his face. "But that's exactly what he'd expect them to do. She kept saying he thinks he's smarter than us. So, what's a twist we wouldn't normally consider? Where else could he possibly take her?" He huffed a breath. "It has to be local. With everyone on high alert, he couldn't have taken her far."

All Gideon could focus on was the futility of them trying to search a hundred different potential locations. They didn't have enough manpower to do that much legwork and he sensed they were running out of time. A sense of paralysis meant he could barely breathe. If he managed to get her out of the state, she'd be lost forever.

Neil looked at him and swore.

"What?"

"He might take him to one of your properties instead. Think about it. Where is the last place he'd expect us to look?"

The random idea offered a bursting sense of hope. "My God. That makes an awful kind of sense." He ran to grab his laptop as Neil explained their theory to Parker. When Gideon returned, he pulled up a long, daunting list of properties.

"Remove anything in the city." Neil began to pace. "I think he'd be too paranoid about being recognized to hold her anywhere that's well-populated. Since his men messed up the last attempt, he'll be hands-on this time."

"That makes sense." His fingers raced to narrow the information down. There were eighteen properties left. "Eighteen left. How else can we reduce the possibilities?"

"Damned if I know."

Tess came to rub Neil's arm. "Come on. Brook thinks like a shrink. This guy's not normal. What warped reasoning would he use to select the perfect place?"

After a moment, he swiveled to stare at her, then turned back to Gideon. "Are there any properties on the list that he wanted to buy and you beat him to the sale?"

Gideon searched his memory, then scanned the list. "Three." He pointed them out.

"We prioritize these three." He called Parker over and explained their thinking.

The lieutenant nodded. "It makes a strange kind of sense. And we're not making any headway with anything else thus far. Let's check into it."

Chapter Sixteen

Within the hour, during which Brook plotted and planned, Ethan returned, carrying a stunning silver evening gown over one arm. "Oh, you're still here, my dear. How fortunate you waited anxiously for me." His sarcasm made her want to vomit as he came to hover over the bed. "Although you look quite delicious lying there, it's important you're dressed to the standard you have recently. So, when I tear this dress off later, I can get the whole tantalizing effect."

"You're a sick son of a bitch."

The warped smile he offered gave her chills. "You have no idea. And, by the way, compliments will get you nowhere." Turning to the guards, he ordered, "Untie her and I'll let you watch her undress. Maybe I'll even give her to you after I'm finished with her." The two men lumbered forward, depraved hunger darkening their eyes. Their leering expressions assured her that any appeal to them for help escaping would go unanswered. One of them released her feet, one her arms, then they stood back once more to gape at her. "Now, take off those tacky clothes."

She stood, glaring at him.

"Defiance won't work in your favor. Quite the contrary." Stepping forward, he slapped her face with enough force she almost toppled over. "I wish I'd remembered to bring some appropriate music to accompany your striptease. You're nothing but another whore, here, not a princess. Do as your master says."

She unbuttoned her shirt slowly to buy some time, but the small delay seemed to have the opposite effect, revving him higher. "Are you trying to tease me? I have an abundant appetite for you, but, who knows, being provocative might earn you some bonus points." Refusing to respond to his taunts, she met his gaze head on, unflinching. He trailed his fingers over her breasts. "Does Gideon suck these or is he above that type of thing?"

Struggling to keep revulsion from her face, she stayed silent.

He pointed to her slacks. "Now, take these off." She slid them down and stepped out of the pool of material on the floor. Stretching to her full height, she stood, waiting. "Turn around." She could feel his lecherous eyes on her, burning a tormented path down her body. "Now, face me." As she reached for the dress, he yanked it out of range of her reach. "Now, now. I don't think my men have had adequate opportunity to relish the delectable sight of you." He turned around, waving them forward. "You really must see what a prime piece of meat looks like. She might be just another gold-digger, but her body is prime real estate." She sensed them ogling her, but refused to meet their hungry expressions. *Show no fear*.

"You see, she thinks she's too good for us, my friends. It's my responsibility to teach her otherwise. There are nights I love my favorite pastime and this is one of them." He tossed the dress to her. "Now, put it on. I'm anxious for our wonderful evening together to begin." She slipped it over her head, feeling the expensive material slither over her body. At least it wasn't snug which would inhibit her movement. Once the dress fell into place, she reached around and struggled with the zipper. Stepping forward to do it up, he paused to run his tongue down her shoulder blade as he did.

Don't get distracted. She stopped herself from gagging. "I need shoes," she stated in as haughty a tone as she could manage. *Heels can be sharp enough to stab someone if you used enough force. All I'd have to do would be to pry off the protective end.*

He chuckled. "Why? We both know shoes can be a weapon. Besides, I like the idea of you being barefoot. Maybe by the end of the night, you'll be both barefoot and pregnant with my child."

The thought caused her stomach acid to brew, but then his words spawned an idea. *Would it serve to throw him off his game?* She met his gaze and smiled. "Too late for that, I'm afraid. Why do you think Gideon bought me a ring?"

****

Gideon's house was filled with frantic activity. Men and women in combat gear and bulletproof vests crowded the kitchen. His home was the closest possible mustering point to all three properties. Desperate to help, Henry kept making huge pots of coffee and offering everyone croissants.

Things had been as orderly and calm as possible until Special-Agent-In-Charge Holstein had shown up. His self-importance seemed to work adversely on the troops. He spoke down to the police officers, but Parker had proven quite adept at distracting him. Finally, he convinced the man to focus on working on preparing a statement for the media. That shuffled him back to his office, getting ready to bask in the limelight; his favorite occupation. When he strutted out the door, everyone seemed to finally concentrate on the plan to save Brook.

The FBI agents seemed quite happy to work with the local police after the removal of their boss, which was a relief. Parker divided the officers into three teams, half agents, half officers, then checked radios and confirmed instructions. The babble back and forth was constant and overwhelming. He, Tess, Neil, and Henry stayed out of the way, not wanting to be an unwelcome distraction. As Parker went through the instructions to his crew, Neil leaned over to Gideon, lowering his voice. "Which of your properties do you think is the most logical choice?"

He paused to consider. "For him, bigger is always better, I'd say the largest one on Stevenson Road. It has many different entrances and the best vantage point to its surroundings."

"I agree with your reasoning." He scanned the room. "As soon as they leave, let's go sit and wait on the side street. That way, if she's there, we're close so we can safely get to her."

"That sounds like an excellent plan."

Three minutes later, the teams all departed. Parker's last words were a promise. "Try not to worry. She knows how to buy us time. We'll get her back safe and sound."

As soon as the teams left, he explained their plan to Tess. "Okay. Let's go," she agreed, jumping up and grabbing her jacket.

He and Neil both insisted, "No. You have to stay here."

Putting her hands on her hips, she glared up at them. "I'm safer with you than I am here. You're not leaving me behind."

"Tess—"

She shook her head, stamping a foot to make her point. "Not in this lifetime. She was my friend first. I'll go with you guys or I'll drive myself." Not wanting to waste precious time on arguing, they reluctantly agreed. Telling Henry they'd be back, they all piled into Brook's car, picking it because it was the least eye-catching of their choices. Neil had his gun holstered and had given his backup to Gideon in case of emergency. He'd become a steady enough shot to hit someone if he had no choice. Ten minutes later, they were parked on the darkest end of Mitchell Road which ran perpendicular to Stevenson.

The waiting proved interminable after only a few dragging minutes. Listening to Neil's radio only yielded signs that guaranteed the assigned team was preparing to enter the property in question. Neil climbed out of the car to check what he could see of the site with the binoculars he'd brought from his bag. He had to stand on the trunk of the car to manage it. At first, he saw nothing, then caught sight of a few team members moving into place, ready the scale the surrounding wall.

For the first time in years, he prayed.

****

Ethan dragged Brook into a large, staged room so bright with light it made her eyes blink and water. On one side, a massive dining table placed next to the wall was set with food and candlelight. On the opposite wall, a large bed had been raised on a wooden pedestal. Cameras were set on all four sides to surround it and powerful stage lights beamed from every corner.

"You see, Brook?" He spread his arms theatrically,

an expression of rampant glee stretching his face. "First, we have a romantic supper to set the appropriate mood, then you can pay for your dinner the old-fashioned way. On your back." He turned to offer a manic grin. "We'll even have an audience. To top off the evening, I'll have the added incentive of shooting some riveting footage with which to torment Gideon. As you can imagine, it will involve a great many closeups." He snickered. "You're going to be a star."

You demented bastard. She lifted her chin. "It's a pretty safe bet you can't compare with him as a lover. At your very best, you'd be a six out of ten. And that's being generous."

"The others screamed," he taunted, his face mottled red with anger. "And so will you."

She shrugged. "I doubt it. You tend to over-estimate the effect you have on me. But I guess you're entitled to your delusions."

He grabbed her and twisted her arm behind her back. "Do you think I won't kill that baby inside you? When I've had my fill, I'll give you to my soldiers and let them do their worst. There'll be nothing left for Gideon but profound loss, heartbreak, and your blood-stained corpse."

His reactive behavior pointed to an upcoming total loss of control. That could only work in her favor. Losing focus on his plan would open the door for an opportunity she could grab. As if her thoughts summoned some assistance, she heard a commotion in the corridor outside the room. The heavy door whipped open, banging against the wall as one of his guards ran inside, panting. "We have intruders. At least four men in combat gear just came over the back wall. I think there's more to follow." She knew they'd find her, but couldn't allow the rush of relief to distract her. The prospect of freedom renewed her resolve.

He shook his fist at the other man, cursing. "Stop them, you idiot, or at least slow them down. Buy me some time." The man ran out, back in the direction he'd come from. Ethan reached into a nearby cabinet and withdrew a pistol. Aiming it at her head, he said, "Move it." Grabbing her arm, he dragged her out the door. He hauled her down a long corridor in the opposite direction the guard had headed. At the end, they trailed to a halt. Unlatching a bolted door with one hand, he pulled it open to reveal a dark, musty tunnel. When they were through the opening, he shut it behind them, latching it so no one could follow. She wondered if he realized he'd cut off any support from the guards as well. He'd abandoned his men without a thought. *Hardly a surprise.*

The two of them stumbled along, banging against the sides as they ran. Soon, they came upon another door. When he yanked it open, she found they were outside the building near a single parked car. The early evening sunlight made her eyes water. He wrenched her arm pulling her through the driver's side door, leaving her behind the wheel. Pointing the gun at her head, he shouted, "Drive!"

Chapter Seventeen

Neil ran to the car, opened the passenger door, and dragged Tess out. "Gideon, we have to take cover." He gestured to the far side of the road. "Hide in the woods. I think Ames and Brook have escaped. I can see a car leaving and heading this way at speed. I have to block the road." He threw himself into the car. Starting the engine, he rammed the vehicle into gear and moved it to block the narrowest part of the road about sixty feet away. Wide ditches on either side would prove impassable. After throwing the vehicle in park, he ran to join the others, shoving Tess to cower behind the biggest tree nearby. "Nobody move until I say it's safe. I might have to shoot him."

"What about Brook?" Panic swamped Gideon.

"He probably has her driving so he can keep a gun on her. When she sees the car, she'll know it's me and that we're nearby."

"Should we call for help?" Gideon muttered, his nerves screaming.

"No time. Trust her. She'll know exactly what she has to do."

****

Brook ignored Ethan's angry curses, concentrating on the road. It was time to bring this to a close before someone got hurt. Namely her. She floored the gas and they hurtled along the road. The coming dark created shadows that didn't help her situation. She would have to ditch the car and control the muzzle of his gun at the same time—no small feat. The late model car guaranteed the presence of air bags, something her safety would depend on. Taking that evasive driving course was, at this moment, the smartest thing she and Neil had ever done.

As if the mere thought of him had conjured up a way out, she saw her car. Jammed in the narrowest spot, it wouldn't be perfect, but she'd make it work. She wouldn't cut her speed until the last moment. Ethan saw the car and, panicking, he made a grab for the wheel. One of her hands clutched the wheel to control it while she stomped on the brakes. The other struggled to force the muzzle of his gun upwards. The last thing she registered before impact was the squealing sound of tires on asphalt.

****

Gideon, Neil, and Tess waited in a shivering huddle, heartbeats throbbing, as ninety agonizing seconds passed. In no time, the sound of an engine accelerating down the road toward them reached their ears. A glare from approaching headlights bounced along the line of trees.

At the last minute, they heard the soprano sound of brakes screaming. A tremendous crash sounded and the car shuddered to a halt, sandwiched against theirs. Shadows played against the wreckage.

"Brook!" Neil yelled. A pale hand came out of the driver's side window and he headed for the opposite side, gun drawn. "Put your hands in the air!"

Gideon saw Neil yank the door open, battling to help control Ames. Telling his sister to stay put, he made a dash for Brook's side of the car. Shoving the door open, he gasped, "Are you okay?"

"Yes, I think so." At her answer, he pulled her free of the air bags. She slid out to rest on the ground nearby, blood trailing down her pale cheek. Next, he checked on Neil, who had Ames under control and was cuffing him. "Tess!" he yelled. "Call Parker!" He returned to cradle Brook in his arms, one hand running over her limbs. "Are you sure you're not injured elsewhere? You have a cut on your head."

"Yes," she answered, her voice shaking. "Just a few scrapes and bruises. Thank God for airbags. The old car died a valiant death." He dropped a kiss on her forehead in response, unwilling to let go of her, even for a moment.

After a minute, Tess scurried over to join them. "T-they're on their way." She crouched beside them, grasping their hands with hers.

They watched Ames stretched out on the ground, cuffed and cursing, as Neil stood over him with his pistol aimed at his chest. A dramatic symphony of sirens screamed in the background, the sounds growing ever closer. When the expected vehicles arrived, men and women in blue spilled from every door. Moments later, they were joined by a team of FBI agents, their logo emblazoned on their bullet-proof vests. As Parker took charge of the scene and sorted things out, Neil held Tess's hand as Gideon checked Brook's injuries to make sure he hadn't missed anything. When he noticed her change in clothes, worry about her experience raised troubling questions in his mind.

Always in tune with him, she read his expression. "He didn't hurt me. He wasted too much time taunting me about you. I egged him on."

He leaned to hug her, murmuring, "Thank God."

They watched as Ethan was led away, screaming curses and fighting every step of the way. Two agents put him in the back of an unmarked car and hurried off, followed by a squad car for added security. Gideon was grateful no media had shown up yet. He had no sooner thought that when he saw a van pull up, the logo of a local station on its side.

Parker walked over. "Things are going to get a little hectic here for a while. I am going to send you folks home for now while I take care of the situation here and at the station. We'll come and take full victim and witness statements, then go over them again first thing in the morning. Brook, do you need to get checked out by the medical staff?"

"No. Just bumps and bruises." She smiled. "I think you're right. We all need to go home." Gideon noticed that she'd referred to his place as home and it warmed him, despite the terrifying hours they'd spent worrying. They were escorted back to the house by one officer. He and the women huddled together in the back seat while Neil sat in the front. Another officer followed to make sure they reached home without any further interference from either the media or the gathering crowd.

When the police cars approached his house, Henry threw open the door, anxiety written all over his face. They spilled out of the packed vehicle and he hustled them inside. Everyone thanked the officers and they departed to return to the scene. They proceeded to the family room, flopping on sofas and chairs. Gideon sighed with relief. "Henry, could you make us some coffee? Parker and his men will be here after they've taken care of things at the scene. I don't think we'll be going to bed anytime soon." He nodded and hurried out, seeming happy to have something helpful to do.

They sat staring at each other, still in shock. Neil sat clutching both of Tess's hands, as if he couldn't bear to let her go. Gideon said to Brook, "Tell us what he did."

"He made me strip in front of the guards and put on this dress. Apparently, he had a 'date' planned with a rather unsettling ending." She tried to soften it, knowing they didn't need to be any more frightened. "He wouldn't give me shoes, saying he wanted me barefoot and pregnant."

Tess sucked in a moan.

She touched Gideon's hand. "I told him he was too late. Why did he think you'd given me a ring?"

"That was a stroke of genius," Neil said. The other two all looked at him, clearly confused. "Well, it distracted him, right? It knocked him off his game."

She nodded. "Yes. It was a calculated risk, but that's when his plan started to fall apart. It enraged him."

"Weren't you scared?" Tess asked.

"Of course, but if you show men like him that you're frightened, that's exactly what they want. They feed off fear. I knew him well enough to not respond with any sign of weakness in order to keep the upper hand."

"Why didn't you karate chop him or whatever?" Tess rubbed her arms. Neil pulled the throw from the back of the couch and tucked it around her shoulders.

"I didn't know how many men were in the house. It made more sense to get outside first, because I was pretty sure he'd leave his men behind. He has no sense of loyalty." She smiled to reassure them. "Right before I saw my car wedged across the road, I was planning how to bring it to an end. You guys gave me an easy way to accomplish that."

"Sorry about your car," Neil said. "It seemed like blocking the road was our most effective strategy."

"I needed to trade it in, anyway," she teased. "It's a small price to pay to have this debacle over and done with."

Parker and another officer appeared an hour later, having left the crime scene in capable hands. He took each one of them aside and took a basic statement so they could retire for the night. The officer also took photographs of Brook's injuries for the file. "We'll have more questions in the morning and we can add any details you've forgotten. I'm afraid your car is a write-off, Brook. I'll give you a form and pictures in the morning that you can forward to your insurance people."

He put an arm around her shoulders and squeezed. "That's the least of our worries, but thanks for taking care of it."

"You're welcome." He grinned. "I kept your boss busy preparing a media statement for the morning. We'll try to get our business finished up before that airs."

"Thanks again, then. I'm not sure I could have borne his posturing after all this." She walked him to the door and said goodnight.

Henry brought a loaded tray with their snacks on it and perched on the ottoman beside them. "Is that the end of this craziness, then? After tomorrow morning, I mean. I think we all need to get back to a little peace and quiet."

Gideon nodded. "It will take a long time before he goes to trial, but our part is over, except for testifying when the time comes. Right?" He turned to Brook for reassurance.

"Yes. Thank goodness. Kidnapping a federal agent is a very big deal. That will buy us enough time to get us access to look for more evidence in the murder case." They talked more, but Tess soon nodded off, slumped against Neil. "Oh, poor thing. I think her adrenaline rush just took a dive."

"I'll take her." He stood and lifted her into his arms. "Goodnight, you two."

They watched as he carried her off. "I do believe Tess might have found her match," Henry said, smiling. "Well, I'm off to bed as well, unless you need anything else."

"No, Henry," Gideon replied. "We're fine. We expect the police back here in the morning to confirm our statements and finish up. Possibly a few agents as well. Perhaps a few extra baked goods might be in order." He sighed. "We won't get much sleep tonight, but I'll make it up to you after they leave."

"Don't worry about that. It will be nice to be able to thank everyone in a way they seem to appreciate." He said goodnight and disappeared through the door.

Gideon looked across at her. "Let's get rid of that awful dress, have a shower, and go to bed."

"Good idea. We'll need to bag it for evidence, then we never have to look at it again."

"Sounds good to me." He stood, holding out his hand. Taking it, she followed him up the stairs.

"My burst of energy from before has finally faded away," she said, dragging her feet across the carpet. "I'm exhausted."

"Me, too. It's a good thing you're the agent. I'm not cut out for such drama and stress." They bagged the dress in a dry cleaner's bag from the closet. Stripping off their clothes, they stepped into the shower together and stood in each other's arms under the heated spray. "I was terrified for you," he murmured, his arms tightening.

"I know. I'm so sorry. All I kept thinking about was how much I would miss out on if I failed."

"Thank you for leaving the trail of jewelry to help us."

"I knew you'd find it, although dumping that beautiful ring in the grass wounded me. For bad guys, they weren't very observant." She kissed him. "Let's finish cleaning up and get to bed." They soaped off and rinsed as quickly as they could.

After toweling them both off, he cleaned her scrapes and bandaged them. In ten minutes, they slipped in between the sheets. Wrapped around each other, they both finally stopped trembling from fear and fatigue. He pulled away for a moment and grabbed her ring from where he'd left it on his nightstand. Slipping it on her finger, he kissed her to stop her objection. "Just keep it on, okay? Everything is going to be all right now." They held each other tight and soon fell asleep.

Chapter Eighteen

In the morning, Brook woke before Gideon did and stared at the ring. Now that this case was more or less finished, she and Neil had some important decisions to make about their future in the agency. And she and Gideon had some plans of a more personal nature to make. It made for a lot of information to have bouncing around in your head this early in the day.

"You think too much," Gideon mumbled. "I can almost hear the gears in your brain turning." She rolled over to face him. His eyes were still closed as she kissed his chest, her hands roaming. "Now, these are enticing activities I can appreciate." He opened his eyes as he reached for her. They made love slowly, touch by touch, sigh by sigh. Climax finally came and carried them into satisfaction. In such a short time, everything had changed for both of them. She felt so much just in the way he looked at her, like she belonged forever at his side. Time would tell if he felt the same, but when she thought about his insistence she wear the ring, she didn't think he would break her heart.

Afterwards, they showered and dressed, feeling lazy, but unsure about when Parker and friends would show up. The clock read eight a.m. When they went downstairs, Henry was making breakfast with the other two nowhere to be found.

"I'll see what's keeping them," Brook said. When

she checked, she found Tess's room empty. The bed hadn't been slept in. With a smile, she peeked into Neil's room. Sure enough, they lay together sleeping, still fully clothed, wrapped around each other. Tess looked tiny curled next to him. She backed out of the room. Turning, she found Gideon behind her. He was smiling. "Let them sleep a while longer," he said. "There's no need to rush. Breakfast can wait."

They had finished their eggs and toast before the others joined them. Tess beamed a smile and looked content. Neil's face flushed when he greeted Gideon, but he relaxed when there were no comments to make him uncomfortable. They finished eating their meal mere moments before Parker showed up with two other policemen. He led them carefully through each of their statements, asking for clarification on a few details. When it came time for Brook's turn, she asked that the others leave. They all looked at her strangely, but complied.

She went on to explain to the professionals. "I didn't want them to know one thing in particular that I didn't mention last night. I'm not sure it's important, but I knew they were coming for me."

Parker looked up from his notes, his gaze narrowing. "Can you explain what you mean?"

"I caught sight of a moved fence panel at the rear of the property. It had been put back in place, but I could see the jagged cut when I checked the fence line. It was important to get Tess out of the way to safety, so I sent her inside on an errand I knew would take a few minutes."

He nodded. "The others might disagree, but, to me, that makes sense. She would have been a liability and at greater risk. With her personality, she would have tried to help, regardless of her own safety. You both might have been injured or killed."

"Exactly. But there's no reason she ever has to know about that. I had to make sure he took me so we'd have enough charges to hold him without bail. As you know, kidnapping a federal agent is always a game changer."

"Fair enough. It was an undeniable risk, but a calculated one and it paid off. Being held on kidnapping a federal officer will allow us time to get all the other charges locked into place. It also allowed us to get the additional warrants we need, too." His phone rang and he answered, listening for a few moments. "Thank you. I wish I could say I'm surprised. I'm almost done here, so I'll be there in about thirty minutes."

Hanging up, he met her gaze. "Your team is leading a search of the property where Gideon was held. A set of human remains has already been discovered and there appears to be more to come. I think you finally got what you need on the original cases." With a triumphant beam lighting his eyes, he paused. "Your boss sent a message that he's far too busy to deal with you today."

"Small loss," she joked. "I think we can deal with our disappointment." Nodding, he strode out the door, chuckling on his way to the scene. Searching for Gideon, she discovered him staring out into the garden. Even with Ethan behind bars, he still hadn't been able to relax. He had tossed and turned most of the night, despite his exhaustion. Moving to stand beside him, she noted his stern expression. "What's wrong?"

"I heard what you said to Parker." There was nothing she could add that would help, so she waited for him to continue. "Part of me wants to thank you for protecting Tess. But the other part wants to wring your neck for risking yourself. Something terrible could have happened."

"It was a calculated risk, Gideon. I realize it's difficult for you to understand, but my job is to assess those on a daily basis. The situation offered an opportunity we weren't going to get any other way. And, bottom line, it worked."

"I was going to go for a walk to help me process all of this, but there are news vans at our gate again, armed with long lenses. Damn voyeurs. Haven't we been through enough?"

She placed a hand on his arm to soothe him. "We promised to focus on the end result, right? The end result is that we're all okay and he's behind bars. And no one's hurt. It's absolutely our best-case scenario."

He smiled. "I guess you're right. You're very good for me, you know. Everything just seems to fall into place when you're near."

She put her arms around his waist. "I'd say that goes both ways."

The four of them played board games all afternoon in an attempt to relax, ignoring the growing crowd of news people shouting for attention outside the gate. Poor Abe just sat and stared at them, growling from time to time. They left the television switched off, exhausted by the endless drama of media coverage. Parker had assigned two policemen to guard the gates until the worst was over. He called Gideon a few times with updates. So far, searchers had found three sets of women's remains and, according to the scanning equipment, there were more to unearth. Ethan had owned the sprawling property there for a dozen years, so where would it end?

How many bodies would they find?

There was only one time that Gideon gave a relaxed smile. He and Neil had returned from a private discussion. He whispered to her about it later, when the others were busy in the kitchen. "He asked me for permission to date Tess. I said, yes, of course. It's nice to finally have something positive to focus on."

The breaking case was splattered all over the newspapers the next day. The one headline they saw read, *Five Bodies and Counting...* Ethan would be transferred to a maximum-security facility tomorrow to await trial. Because of his money and the long string of crimes they suspected him of, the judge considered him a serious flight risk. There would be no bail and he was under heavy guard. For once, the wheels of justice were working as they should.

When she and Neil discussed moving back to their apartments, Gideon raised his hand in a stopping motion. "Can we stay here together until everything calms down a bit? After that, we can figure out how we all want to move forward."

"That's no hardship for us," Neil replied, darting a glance at Tess who grinned in response. Brook nodded her agreement, unable to deny her preference to stay at her lover's side.

Their boss, Special Agent In Charge Holstein, showed up to meet with Gideon and pretty much took all the credit for catching Ames. Gideon looked less than impressed, but managed to be civil while Brook tried to keep a straight face. Their boss was probably shown the door a little quicker than he'd counted on when he took the time to drive over. Afterwards, Gideon cooked dinner for all of them, a huge beef casserole with cheesy noodles, the best kind of comfort food. Tess baked cookies for dessert while Neil kept her company. To relax, they watched an old musical on DVD. It was almost spooky how at home they all felt together.

The next morning, the aggressive news crowds had mostly disappeared, tired of being shut out. Gideon noted that the two policemen were gone, likely called to assist with another case. Brook, Gideon, and Neil were together in the kitchen when her telephone rang. It was Parker. She listened to what he had to say, hung up, and turned to Gideon. "Get Henry inside. Now." He hurried out to the garden, hollering his name.

"What's wrong?' Neil asked.

"The jail transfer van was intercepted. Four masked men shot the guards and took Ethan with them. They're worried he might be headed here. Help is on the way."

Henry and Gideon returned. She saw Tess was missing. "Where is Tess?"

"Upstairs," Neil answered. "I'll get her." He hustled out the kitchen door.

"We need to stay together until they catch them," she said. "Let's check the doors. I'll get the front."

While Henry and Gideon did the back entrances, she followed Neil's path out the kitchen door. Rounding the corner of the hall, she came to a skidding halt. Neil stood in front of her, stock still, his back to her. Confused, she peered past him. Across the large foyer, Tess stood, pale and shaking, Ethan's arm around her throat. He had a gun aimed at the side of her forehead. "Well, well. Looks like the gang's all here. What fun."

"Let her go." Brook started to calculate distances from where she stood to where her friend was being held.

"That's not likely, is it?" The maniacal grin on his

face chilled her.

"She has nothing to do with this." Brook stepped in front of Neil to distract Ethan and then continued slightly to one side as his eyes tracked her movements.

"I'd say she has everything to do with this. Just another uppity little bitch who thinks she's too good for me."

She forced her voice to stay calm, despite her mounting fear for her friend's safety. "I'll swap places with her. I'm more valuable to you as a hostage than she is."

He laughed. "I think I'll keep her, thanks. You were a massive disappointment, to say the least. What is it they say about frauds? All frosting and no cake?"

She heard Henry and Gideon enter from behind Neil. "Stay back there," she ordered them without turning around. She watched in her peripheral vision as they did as she instructed. "The police are on their way."

"They won't reach here in time. I promise. The streets are blocked with cars, most of them full of officers looking for me. Ironic, isn't it? As always, they're just a little too slow." He tightened his hold, making Tess gasp. "You should have known that you couldn't beat me at my own game."

He took a pace back toward the door as Neil coughed. "Tess, down," she shouted.

Tess let her weight drop toward the floor the necessary few inches as Neil's shot sounded. The bullet hit Ethan square in the forehead. He fell, sprawling, on top of Tess as she crumpled to the floor.

Neil hurtled past Brook to push Ames's body off Tess, grabbing her and pulling her away to shield her eyes. Brook kicked the gun to the side, checking Ethan's pulse to be certain there was no sign of life. "He's gone." She looked at Neil cradling Tess as she sobbed, clutching his shirt. "It's okay, Tess. Everyone's all right." Her words couldn't take away the enormous shock, but she'd recover with some help.

Glancing at Gideon's pale face, she said, "Call Parker. Tell him we're okay." Sirens wailed, and she looked out the window to see armed men racing across the lawn. *Do they already have Ames's men?* "He's probably close." A few moments later, as word of their safety spread, everyone lowered their weapons and entered the vestibule. They stood quietly and listened to orders as the group of police officers took over the scene. When they tried to separate them, Neil refused to leave Tess's side and Gideon followed suit.

The few news people who remained at the gate found out too late about what had happened under their very noses. Their first clue had been the line of police cars that came rushing down the road, roof lights wheeling to accompany the blaring sirens.

Inside and out, the property became a circus with different acts in every corner. The five of them were permitted to sit together on the couches in the family room while the police, medical examiner, and evidence team came to carry out their duties. Parker even arranged for a cleanup team to come in late the following day after the evidence and photographs had been taken and they had time for a final look. Still in shock, the five of them said little unless asked. Finally, Henry was allowed to get up and make a big pot of coffee, commenting that he knew everyone would be working for a while. Brook asked if she could help, but he waved her away.

They remained together this time as they gave

Parker their statements. Their boss came and collected Neil's gun, pending investigation, as required by the bureau. Tess rushed to his defense before he told her this was normal in the event of a shooting death that involved one of their agents.

At midnight, after an exhausting day, the house finally cleared out. Parker was the last to leave. His final words were, "It's more efficient this way. No one will ever have to fear him again and it won't cost a fortune to prosecute him. We'll go after all the underlings he hired now and ensure the victims' families finally get some peace."

Gideon seemed shocked at his unemotional attitude, but she explained that cops tend to look at the more practical aspects of crime in order to stay sane. It helped them to handle all the emotional repercussions of their work. Otherwise, the constant drama of it all would be unbearable. Exhausted, they all finally retired to their bedrooms. She stayed with Gideon. They barely managed a mumbled goodnight before they fell asleep and finally slept for hours.

In the morning, they were sitting at the kitchen table, discussing the traumatic events of the previous day, when her cellphone interrupted them. She saw to her shock that it was Holstein's boss, the man they jokingly referred to as "The Big Cheese."

"Good morning, sir." She listened to his request, then asked for a moment, covering the phone. "May Neil and I have a meeting with our senior advisor here this morning?"

"Certainly," Gideon answered.

"Yes, sir. That's fine. We'll see you at eleven." She hung up.

Gideon looked concerned. "What's that all about?"

Her head still foggy from sleep, she looked at her partner, shrugging. "I don't have a clue. Do you?"

"Nope. Did he sound pissed?"

"Not at all. He congratulated us on catching Ames and said that we needed to talk asap."

They decided they were too tired to worry about it and spent the intervening time trying to relax. When the big boss arrived, he had his four-man security detail wait outside. They used the formal dining room as a stand in conference room for their meeting. Once they were seated, he offered an official thank you for their actions in getting such a lengthy, difficult case closed. "Thank you, sir." Brook always spoke for the both of them. Neil was a little paranoid about dealing with the top brass.

"I have heard rumblings around the agency that you two are considering giving up your field jobs and moving on."

She glanced at Neil and, when he nodded his permission, she responded. "We've recently been considering our options. Neil and I have been in the field for fifteen years and find ourselves interested in considering a safer job with more stable work hours."

"I can understand that, especially after working a complex case like this for so long." He steepled his fingers. His calm demeanor, gleaming gray hair, and spotless suit made him seem more like a therapist than a director of the FBI. "We would hate to lose you, though. You both have exemplary records and have from the very beginning of your careers."

"Thank you, sir."

"I'm wondering if I could interest you in serving in an advisory capacity to the teams. We're working on some restructuring of this entire division, something that is long overdue. It came to my attention that you two seem to have a proclivity for reducing the excess in any plan. Right now, that's exactly what we need. Every year, we struggle with a shrinking budget. Cutting to essential personnel and materials is a strategy that saves us money and allows us some latitude in taking on additional cases we otherwise wouldn't have the time or the financial support to handle."

Neil finally spoke up with one question that was on both of their minds. "Where would that put us in terms of Special Agent Holstein, sir?" *Leave it to Neil to cut to the chase.*

The director looked amused and Brook intuited from his expression that the news of Holstein's poor management style had reached the top brass. "Holstein is being transferred to another division where, to be brutally frank, I hope he will be more effective. I trust your discretion will keep that bit of news between the three of us for now." At their agreement, he continued. "These two positions would be above his level anyway and wouldn't involve any fieldwork unless there was gross mis-handling involved. You two would work as equals, advising the teams on how best to accomplish their goals." He met their gazes one, then the other, as if to gauge their interest. "You would also review the strategy used after every case to determine effectiveness and implement any necessary changes for the future. It would be pretty close to a nine to five, Monday to Friday setup."

She and Neil would need some time to review their options. "Your offer sounds interesting. May we have some time to think about it?"

"Of course. I wanted to talk to you now because I didn't want you two resigning before you knew what we could offer." He stood. "Shall we say a week to take some down time and mull it over? And come to see me personally when you have your answer. I'll advise my secretary to wait for your call."

"That's more than fair, sir. Thank you." He added a few necessary details, mentioning an increase in pay and added benefits in hopes of tempting them into acceptance. After that, they saw him out, trying to ignore the almost comic curiosity on Tess and Gideon's faces. After the door closed behind him, they clustered around. Returning to the kitchen table, they each took a seat while Brook explained what had happened.

"Oh, my gosh." Tess vibrated in place, her excitement impossible to contain. "Do you think you'll take it?"

"We'll certainly consider it. He's going to have human resources email a more detailed package this afternoon. From what he indicated, it should be a reasonable raise, at least. And we have a week to decide."

"Would you be based here?" Gideon asked.

"Yes. They're re-structuring the unit and moving to a bigger building." He and Tess looked at each other, grinning.

A great deal happened in the next three weeks in terms of positive progress. When all was said and done, they found a total of fourteen bodies on Ethan's land. She and Neil spent the remaining time in their current jobs helping to identify the bodies. Surprisingly, not all the remains were female. It seems that, years ago, Ethan had bumped off a few rivals along his career path. No one had ever connected those deaths to him. It still made her shudder to think that one of them could have been Gideon.

She and Neil accepted their new positions at the FBI. They would move into the new building in six months and finally have decent-sized offices and a new challenge to enjoy. In the meantime, they would be transitioning from one position to the other. Their old boss had been removed and replaced with a much more talented female version. He was said to be most unhappy with the turn of events. Apparently, he had expected to be named as boss of the new unit.

Neil had moved back to his apartment, but he and Tess were officially dating. He spent more time with her than he did at home. Brook had never seen him so content.

At Gideon's urging, she gave up her plain-Jane apartment and moved into the house with him and Tess. She brought her paltry wardrobe, a few personal things, and donated the rest to charity. It still astonished her how much she felt at home in her new surroundings.

Tonight, they were all lounging at the house until Tess and Neil disappeared to the back yard. She watched their dim shadows by the pagoda. "They're so happy together."

Gideon came to join her, putting an arm around her waist. "When all this mess started, I could have never envisioned such a fantastic outcome, could you?"

"Never. I'm afraid I'm far too practical to have that good of an imagination."

"I'm proud of us for having made it through in one piece." He kissed her cheek. "Thanks to you two, of course."

"We all did our part." She chuckled. "You'll never guess what I heard today."

He lifted his eyebrows. "What's that?"

"You remember our old boss?"

Smirking, he said, "The appropriately named misogynist A Hole?"

"Yes. They're shifting his new position so that he'll be reporting to the recently-appointed female director of the unit. And I heard she doesn't suffer fools easily." She couldn't hold back a broad grin. "I guess, from time to time, justice really does prevail."

A word about the author...

Dianne McCartney is an award-winning writer, speaker, and contest judge from Canon City, Colorado. She lives with her husband, Mitch, among the deer, coyotes, and other wildlife. Her novels are mainstream thriller/suspense and contemporary romance published by The Wild Rose Press. She has sixty-eight writing awards from contests in Oklahoma and Texas and is a member of the OWFI, The Rose Rock Writers, The Tornado Alley Mystery Writers, and The Oklahoma Romance Writers' Guild.

http://www.diannemccartney.com

Thank you for purchasing
this publication of The Wild Rose Press, Inc.

For questions or more information
contact us at
info@thewildrosepress.com.

The Wild Rose Press, Inc.
www.thewildrosepress.com

www.ingramcontent.com/pod-product-compliance
Lightning Source LLC
Chambersburg PA
CBHW060103260626
47160CB00005B/1785